Waiting for Sunrise

Heather Keleher

ISBN: 1936731010
ISBN-13: 978-1-936731-01-5

For My Wonderful Family

NIGHT

Chapter One

The light of day melted into the dark expanse of ocean, velvety curtain of night falling across glimmering stage of sky. I leaned against the fogged glass of the plane's window, peering out as the sun bowed to her captive audience. She curtsied, the rainbow drape of her dress swirling around her as she ceded her much-applauded role to the satin moon. Watching the exchange from my transcendent front-row view, a slow smile spread across my face. I rested my hand over my rounded stomach, sensing movement from the baby inside, and smiled slightly at the beautiful, butterfly feeling of pregnancy. The crackling of an announcement from the pilot shook me from my thoughts and I shivered for a moment, plunging back into the recluse of my mind in the static silence that followed. My smile wavered, joy distorted in the tumultuousness of the last month. I closed my eyes, and it was December 4th, 2009 again.

~ My eyes flickered open; cotton-strand rays of sunlight filtered through pale curtains, light lazily streaming across my husband, Aaron. I stretched to kiss him; my cheek touched his, meeting cold flesh. "Aaron?" I asked, voice vibrating with the hum of sleep, "Aaron?" Silence hung heavy, drifting, settling in the space between us. Throbbing pulse echoing in me, fingers clenched onto the taut wrinkles of cotton across his breast, I gasped, "Aaron!" My ragged breathing tore out of me as I felt his chest for movement. Shaking, my hand hovered above his mouth and nose, sensing for the soft breath of sleep, "Aaron!" Trembling, I grabbed a phone from the side of our bed, my fingers stumbling to press the digits 9-1-1, "My husband isn't breathing, please come quickly." I touched his cheeks with unsteady hands, clenched his arms with fearful force, "Aaron, please wake up, wake up!" Hot tears rushed down my face, dark blots staining his shirt. "Aaron!" I sobbed, "Aaron!" My hands twisted his shirt and my head fell onto his chest, the repetition of his name distorted in the film of material.

I swallowed, throat aching dry with fear, as medics studied him. My eyes flitted over his body, his light eyelashes flat against colorless cheek, black pajama pants limp on long legs, blonde hair pushed across unlined forehead. I clamped my eyes shut, head reeling. "Please, oh God please," I whispered; they were louder than any words I had ever spoken, resounding through my head and filling my body with their buzz. My eyes fluttered open as a woman with kind eyes came towards me and murmured, "He's gone, I'm very sorry." My lips shuddered and eyes closed, body racked with sobs.

"Our baby. Oh God no." I stumbled onto the bed, quaking hands stroking his collarbone, tracing his jawline. My voice broke, "Aaron, don't leave me." A sheet of tears obscured my vision, light shimmering in a haze. Memories flashed through my head, roaring with pain. In that raw daze, we met for the first time in second grade, eyes darting towards each other and then away … We danced together at a school dance in eighth grade, a smile of excitement enveloping my lips, nerves evident in his blue eyes … He kissed me for the first time on the street outside my parents' condo, standing under the foggy glow of the street lamp on a day more a dream than reality … We gleefully tumbled down the front stairwell of the cathedral, white rice flying and bells joyously singing for our life together at our wedding … The two of us sang to lively, crackling songs on our record player, dancing the Charleston in our small kitchen, bumping into corners and laughing as we did…

My eyes burst open, our past a dream and our future dead.

The medic put her hand on my shoulder; I shook her off. I brushed Aaron's hair back into place and ran a finger across his cheekbone. My voice tore, "Aaron, Aaron." ~

My wet eyes fluttered open, finding my cheek pressed against lifeless glass. A tear shuffled down my face as I stared into the blackness beyond. The liquid expanse of night flooded the Earth in a primeval torrent. I turned off the light above my head and the rhythmic flow of the darkness surrounded the plane, lulling me back into my past.

~ In the days prior to Aaron's funeral, I lay in bed, the crinkled sheets as rough as butcher's paper against my body and the pillow hardly more than a wooden chopping block, tossing, turning, searching, trying to make reality disappear and slowly falling into sweet denial.

On the third night after his death, I sat in the kitchen with my parents, who had abandoned their own lives to help me gather the shards of mine. I heated three mugs of hot chocolate and rested at the glistening granite counter, wrapped up tightly in Aaron's plush robe. The faint smell of his cologne wafted around me and I closed my eyes, letting it seep into me, knowing that a day would come when that shadowy smell would disappear altogether into the void where he had gone. My dark brown hair obscured my face, as I stirred the hot chocolate, watching the final swirling grains of dissent dissolve into nothingness. My hand spun the spoon around and around as if by its own accord. I sipped the hot chocolate silently and felt the burning liquid blister the roof of my mouth. The scorching sensation gave me something to hold onto, a lifesaver in that tempestuous sea churning around me. My heart numbed in the wintery darkness of my mind, throbbing as the waves of grief ebbed and flowed. The room was cast in dusk, ghosts of shadows creeping across the walls. Faint sirens beckoned, voices hurled into the air in a symphony of horns and wails. Headlights on the streets below blinked, flashing like twin stars in a final burst of glory, fizzling out, vanishing into oblivion.

The next morning, I stood under the searing water of the shower, wilted head bowed forward, body stalwart. I dressed with limp fingers and walked downstairs to meet Aaron's parents, Stacy and John: red-tinged eyes, creased foreheads, and tearstains hollow on their cheeks. I suppressed a sob as I wrapped my arms around them. I ran a shuddering hand over my unruly curls, "I'm so sorry. I miss him so very much." Stacy took my hand and stroked it with quivering palm. I looked into her tired eyes and closed mine for a moment, "Stacy. John. Aaron and I had wanted to tell you something together and I know that he would want you to know it now." Stacy tilted her head against her shoulder, stricken with the weight of her grief, "What is it darling?" My lips twitched upwards as I said, "Aaron and I are going to have a baby." Stacy gasped and burst into fresh tears as she took me in her arms once more, "Oh Nicolette, how beautiful."

The days after his funeral passed blurred into a mess of sorting and sifting through the fragments of our life. The debris of memories drifted around me like flinty stars. With the time off from my job at Zola, a fashion design company, my feeling of purposelessness mounted. Callouses hardened my hands as I cleaned and organized and cleaned, sifting through the house with the cool chill of winter at my back and restless fingers smoothing the same crisp linens, straightening the same weathered books, wiping the same pristine counters.

The streets of Christmas danced, flurries of snow twirling across Central Park and sugar-dusting the buildings of the city. Children leapt from their beds, noses pressed against the windows, excited breath fogging the glass. I stepped out onto the street towards the restaurant where my family was meeting for Christmas brunch. I hurried into the restaurant, kissing and hugging my twin brother, Mitch, his girlfriend Char, and my sister, Amelia, and her three children.

After brunch we crowded around the fire in my parents' condo, passing presents out to the children. As they ran squealing and tossing shredded wrapping paper in the air like confetti, the adults looked on with joking consternation and light laughs that flitted to the ceiling as flightily as the snow fell outside. After the little ones had gone off to play with their new dolls and stuffed animals, we passed out presents in a relaxed manner dissimilar to the chaotic giddiness of the children. When all of the festively wrapped presents had been gifted, I found one in my hands with a simple tag in careful script:

"For our Nicolette. With all of our love, your family."

I gently tore the holly berry printed-paper and found a beautifully engraved, deeply colored maple wood box. I cautiously lifted the lid; inside lay a long, thin sheet of tissue paper. I picked it up and a piece of paper fluttered into my lap with the precision and grace of a dove. My hand flew to my lips as I stared at it: a ticket to Milan, Italy with a voucher for a rental car to drive to Florence. My family members smiled softly and I enveloped them in a hug, "Thank you so much! Thank You!" My eyes flooded and I bowed my head into my hands, laughing and crying. ~

The blare of an announcement on my flight woke me once more to find the sky turning bright pink with the blush of sunrise. The pilot announced that there were approximately two more hours in the duration of our flight to Milan. I grinned as I stared out onto the unfamiliar landscape of Europe: mountain peaks dancing upwards in swirls of snow – twirled piles of powdery meringue arrayed in a bakery window, blindly rushing rivers, and sheet cake patches of land frosted with the softest icing of snow. My mind drifted from the European continent, fluttering away a thousand miles.

~ In the last days of December, I arrived at my doctor's office and waited in a pale yellow waiting room. My Ob/Gyn, Dr. James, came in and greeted me with a kind smile. We walked into a small examination room. He stepped out while I lay down on the bed and a nurse entered and talked to me about how I felt and confirmed my May 10th due date. Finally Dr. James returned with a monitor; I pulled my shirt over my stomach so that a nurse could rub on a clear, cool gel. They placed the ultrasound probe on my belly over the gel. Suddenly, a picture came onto the screen. My heart skipped a beat as I looked at my baby, alive and well within me. "Nicolette, you are going to have a little girl," Dr. James exclaimed after looking at the screen. The joy and grief whirled within me, pooling in my chest; Aaron and I had dreamed of having a daughter. I stared at the screen, the shadow of life emerging from the darkness that surrounded me. Happiness bubbled in my chest, pushing up the choking sadness. My breathing came out in stops and starts as my eyes closed, the cool refuge of tears running down my hollowed cheeks. I was so happy to see our baby, but a cascade of other emotions poured into my joy, distorting it into something unrecognizable.

I gently prodded the ultrasound picture of our daughter into a picture frame, stopped at a Bodega for a vase of daisies, and hailed a cab to go somewhere that I had been afraid to go before.

I arrived at the cemetery thirty minutes later and stumbled across the snow-obscured land to Aaron's grave. I knelt, the snow seeping through my black pants, "Hi Aaron, I wanted you to be the first to see the picture of our baby girl. I love you and I miss you." It turned into a single sentence of swallowed tears, "It's so hard to live without you. I love you and I can't go a minute without thinking about you. I wish that I could be talking to the real you right now because you would hug me and hold me and tell me that everything is okay." Tears strangled me, gripping my throat with their greed. "Aaron, our love was so amazing and real and beautiful. You were so young." I put the daisies in front of his gravestone, rocking back and forth, hugging myself. "These are for you, to brighten things up, you always did hate dark places," I then placed the framed ultrasound beside the daisies, "This is our baby, our baby girl." I sat pensively for a long time, wiping the tears from my face, resting my head in the nest of my hands, and then I slowly stood and stepped towards the waiting cab.

Slipping off my shoes with a sad calmness in my green eyes, I lay down on our bed, staring at the white expanse of ceiling, then let my eyes fall shut until I could picture Aaron next to me. The imprint of his body in the bed hovered, a shadow of a reality twisted beyond measure. But illusions can only last so long. My eyes flew open and I peeked at the actuality of my life through shrouded vision, staring for a moment at my beautiful white-gold wedding ring, which twisted in a vine-like way around my slender finger, embedded with twinkling diamonds. Aaron's ring, a simple golden ring with little vines etched on it, was given to me before he was buried and I had strung it on a gold chain around my neck. My daughter stirred inside me and a small smile spread across my face. With bittersweet thoughts about the past and the hope of the future inscribed within, I fell asleep with the ghost of a smile hovering on my lips.

In the darkness of my sleep, dreams came later than normal. Most nights, the twists and turns of my dreams were haunted with the future that had been irrevocably changed, but that day, Aaron appeared, stepping towards me, and wrapped his arms around me. His misty touch traced my wrists and moved up my arms. "I love you." The words fluttered in a whispered voice and within an instant, he diffused into mist and the wind spread the last particles of him away from me. ~

Eyes cleared from the whispers of the past, I yawned, stretching out my tired limbs. As the wheels of the plane touched down onto the runway, my heart sped up.

Chapter Two

Waiting in line for customs, I tapped my feet with bright anticipation. The customs officials, adorned in crisp dark blue uniforms, stamped the passports in a relaxed manner. After the monotonous song peppered with the rustle of pages and definitive thump of the stamp looped for several minutes, I stood next in line. The official yawned with a half smile, looked at my passport, and picked up the stamper limply. In an Olympic feat he scanned the little novel of my travels, swiping it in a gesture that can most kindly be described as lackadaisical and then smiled widely as he handed it back.

Beautiful fields stretched leisurely across the landscape and the sweet Italian breeze trickled through the partially open window of the car, tickling my cheeks. I watched the weathered walls of the Italian villas and the crumbling façades of ancient cities pass in a blur. The snow-capped mountains formed the backdrop to every sight until every so often, a tunnel or bridge would obstruct the picturesque scene. The river Arno flowed through 'Bella Toscana,' her barely moving ripples guiding me to the end of my journey. When the proud buildings of Florence appeared and the Ponte Vecchio was close enough to touch, my heart skipped a beat.

I checked in to the Lungarno Suites with a softly smiling Italian lady who led me up to my one bedroom suite. After she left, I spun around, the world blurring in a perfect haze, and fell onto the bed.

I woke up the next morning to the chattering voices of Italians mingling on the street below, and the sun streaming through the panes of glass. Strolling down a main street sprinkled with pigeons, boutiques, and gelaterias, a tantalizing smell whipped around me. Turning my head both ways, seeking, I practically floated towards a stand where a young woman in a starched black apron served Nutella drenched waffles. I bought one and wandered down the street. It was an almost divine moment as the ambrosial, buttery waffle melted in my mouth and dissolved to crystal flakes on my tongue. I closed my eyes as I tried to capture the memory of the chilly air disrupted by warm blasts of Nutella scented wafts.

Placated with a full stomach, I wandered into the winding streets of Florence. My shoes slipped and slid as I tripped along over the cobblestones, luxuriating in the blissful fact that I had completely left the world I knew. I took in every brick, every stroke of paint on the buttercup yellow buildings, every pillar testament to the survival of this city, every rush of heat from a passing store – the heavy scent of leather wafting into the thin coldness of the day. I stumbled across a market square featuring a fountain with a hog, whose gold nose gleamed brightly against a bronzed body, spitting water out of his gaping mouth in inconsistent spurts. The square brimmed over with life. The forceful pushing and shoving of the vivacious Italians and smiling tourists made me laugh – a sound I had nearly forgotten.

I found myself propelled towards a cart with gorgeous woolen shawls. The rich wools were deep and velvety, warming my color-loving soul. I let my hand gently hover over the resting fabric as if it were too holy to touch. In a light motion, I ran my hand across the wool and forced myself not to pluck one of the shawls up and run the smooth fabric across my cheek. In the halting Italian I'd learned in high school, I asked the artisan, an old woman with gnarled hands, the price of her goods. I watched her face light up in a gummy smile as her needles click-clacked away and she said in Italian too slow to be natural for a native, that it was twenty euros. Then in a conspiratorial undertone she laughed, "But for you, it is ten euros." I purchased a soulful heather-lilac colored shawl with a unique design with a bright, "*Grazie mille!*"

Ambling away from the market, I spotted a café on a side street and strolled in, my throat aching with cold, wiping the flakes of Italian snow off of my shoulders. I ordered a white hot chocolate and smiled with a childlike pleasure as I sipped it slowly out from a heat soaked ceramic mug. I slipped out of my coat and placed a hand over my growing stomach, stretching out my back as I dreamed of bringing my little girl to Italy someday in the future. As I looked up again from my reverie, I noticed a man looking at me with a small smile on his face. He had curly, dark brown hair, knowing brown eyes, and an ageless face. Upon seeing that I had spotted his glance, the man peered back into his newspaper with a smile still hovering in his eyes. I finished my hot chocolate and hurried back into the cold, knotting the belt of my jacket.

My dreams that night were filled with laughter and a vision of Aaron, our daughter, and me together in Florence. When I woke from the sweet solace of my dream, I felt a bittersweet pang in my heart. Morning sickness interrupted my routine yet again as my eyes slid shut, waves of nausea rippling and head pounding with each beat of my heart. I stood there after my shower with a hand spread across my broadened belly, thinking of my child within.

I meandered onto the street with a Nutella waffle in my hand – sure the baby was enjoying it as much as I was. The saccharine clumps of sugar melted oh so dreamily and swirled in an exotic tango with the scrumptious Nutella. As I took the last bite, my taste buds clamored for more.

I had my day planned out to perfection, with a stop to see each of the three David's that Florence claimed her own. My first stop was the Palazzo Vecchio. Front and center in the plaza stood a statue of David. He guarded the palace of bricks colored varying shades of brown, securing with naught but sling and stone an arched doorway with a midnight blue mosaic of golden fleur-de-lis shielded by miniature prowling lions on pedestals.

Off to the side, on a platform, abided sculptures of famous heroes facing trials and goddesses doling protection. Against the wall, draped in stony, flowing robes stood the goddesses, hands lightly arrayed in gestures of defense, legs tilted, and hips swung to the side. Bronzed Mercury stood proudly atop the body of Medusa, holding forth her dripping head in offering to the tourists. Perseus straddled a centaur, striking down with mirth in his eyes and club in his hand. Menelaus, his eyes piercing into the crowd, staggered with the support of a dying, limp Patroclus. Two Medici lions, with cascading curls, picture ready smiles, and veined marble legs, rested their careful paws on balls, guarding the precious statues under the pillars of the Loggia dei Lanzi. I perched myself on a chilly bench and took out my sketchbook while a Russian guitarist, with wares of c.d.'s tenderly placed on a blanket, filled the cool air with stands of music.

When I was a child, I dreamed of becoming an artist, yet, as I grew older, I realized a life of art would be tumultuous and pursued stability. Aaron painted in his spare time from being a lawyer; I loved to sketch whenever I could and with even this small amount of art in my life, I was content. Since Aaron was gone, there were to be no more thick oil and soft watercolor paintings of me or of his serene naturalistic scenes. My dreams of art began to haunt me with questions of what life could have been.

As I picked up my sketchbook and felt the crisp papers under my soft hands, I felt my passion rekindled. I rolled the soft charcoal pencil across my bare palm and shivered with delight at the thick, powdery mark it left on my hand. I started to draw, slowly, deliberately, with the concentration of a scholar to her books. Slowly and surely a picture emerged out of the lines. When I finished, I peered up at the statue and then at the drawing and found that they were very much alike. Once my sketchbook was tucked safely back into my purse, I left the palazzo with plans to return.

I followed the winding pedestrian streets to the Accademia di Belle Arti di Firenze, or more affectionately, The Accademia, where the original David stands. Moving quickly past Michelangelo's giants emerging from stone and painted saints in alternating postures of benediction and suffering, I encountered what I had sought. I stood in awe at the marble giant standing in front of me. My first thought was that of his great height, standing seventeen feet tall in precise marble. His face held a multitude of emotions: he was young and scared, but courage was strong in his large almond shaped eyes. His muscles rippled and his intricate curly hair twisted and turned with the detail that only a master could achieve. Hands and feet slightly too large for his body exhibited his silent power. I could only imagine the sensation he evoked in the time that Michelangelo first sculpted David's innocent beauty, so unafraid of the harsh world ahead of him. I perched on a bench, bent forward, intent in my examination of the masterpiece. I watched him in his serenity, the flurry of tourists surrounding him akin to dwarfs in his shadow. He seemed to look down at them with that impassive face, a secret laugh heaving in his chest at their stares and awe.

With one final David to see, I crossed the Ponte Vecchio, my feet beginning to ache with the lengths of walking the city. I marched up the steep stairs to the Piazzale Michelangelo where a few restaurants, many vendors, myriad tourists, and my last David of the day stood. He stood against the sky, greened by time, carefully surveying his creator's precious city. Whirligig scarves danced in circles around each other, a joyous May Dance in January wind under the refuge of a stand. I stood by a long, curved railing, looking across the vast landscape. The dome of the Duomo peaked above the gold-lit buildings, proudly stubborn in its magnitude, resolute against the ages – a stronghold of the past. Mountains softly rippled and surged against the sky, a navy haze in the light of sunset. The sun glinted falling from the sky, as if gently dropping into the streets to greet a vendor or two, nibble on a biscotto, perhaps sit for a moment, resting on the Duomo, and wander slowly back into the sky.

I entered a family owned restaurant where I ordered a deliciously hearty lentil soup with sultry flavors of paprika and curry tangled in the mix. As the last bites disappeared, washed down with a bubbly San Pellegrino, I sighed contentedly and settled back in my chair in the laid back manner of an Italian to wait for the check.

The air was blue with dusk and the dulcet strains of a guitar floated towards me, hovering, pulsating in the wind. I tugged my knit cap off, raked a hand through my tousled curls, and shoved the cap into my purse. The music pulled me forward and I found myself enveloped in its tender notes. The signs and CDs in the velvet draped guitar case in front of the musician read 'Claudio Spadi.' Strands of people surrounded me on the pavement of the Ponte Vecchio, tourists and natives of Florence alike, drawn together by the music. As I sat there, listening to Duran Duran's 'Save a Prayer,' I let the thoughts I had been holding back about life and love come back to me and pondered them. I thought of Aaron, who should have been sitting beside me, listening to the music and wrapping his arms around me to keep away the cold. Bittersweet tears slipped down my face. As the moon rose higher in the sky and its light gently illuminated the Arno, I pulled myself away from the guitar's sweet sounds and walked in a fog to the hotel.

I woke up to a small alarm that I barely remembered setting and pulled myself away from the embrace of the sheets, recalling that I had scheduled a Tuscan cooking class for that day. I walked out of my suite and to the street where I met the guide and other 'cooks.' One was a young American woman, just a few years younger than me, who was taking a year off college to travel. The second and third were a middle-aged man and his wife from Sweden. The last one in the class, oddly enough, was the man from the café two days before. He was a friend of the head chef and spoke English with a strong accent. Leonardo was his name, or rather Leo, and he was an astronomy professor at the University of Florence. He struck up a conversation with me, laughingly saying that he had wanted to learn how to cook something instead of purchasing precooked food or depending on his sister to bring him meals. By the time the guide had appeared, we were chatting like old friends.

Our group strolled along the charming streets, the fluorescent-lit shops and the speeding Vespas dancing with the aged quaintness of the buildings and streetlamps across the delicate line of change. Perfectly intermingling segments of old and new flowed throughout the city, boundless and sourceless. After arriving at the market, we gaped at the magnificent selection available, purchasing different ingredients and sampling tangy vinegars and fragrant olive oils with crusty cubes of bread. Silvery rain danced around us as we ventured to our kitchen; the petite droplets made serene music against the rainbow of bright umbrellas that were held by the little crowds wandering down the street.

At a small apartment with a marvelous kitchen, each cook was put in charge of a different course – I made the dessert, a creamy tiramisu – and together we created a fabulous meal. We ate the delightful food together around the kitchen counter and left the apartment with indulgent smiles spread across our faces. Leo invited me for a cup of coffee at his favorite café, the café where I had seen him for the first time.

We spoke intently and quietly about our ambitions. Time passed quickly and he finally asked the question that I had been braced for from the start of our conversation. "If I might ask without being disrespectful, Nicolette, where is your husband? I can see you are with child and you wear a wedding ring." My face fell, "Well, he died in December. I'm pregnant with our daughter." My eyes glazed as I stared blankly ahead and Leo placed his hand on mine, "I'm so sorry." We stood and Leo asked if he could walk me back to the Lungarno Suites. I agreed and as we made our way through the cold, he told me about the book he was writing. As we reached the Suites, I waved goodbye and he smiled, eyes laughing, and disappeared into the maze of streets.

I woke late and sat perched on my bed with my legs folded under me, peering out the window at the shining sun. Closing my eyes, I drifted towards the window and leaned against its sill, the cold from outside barred from me, yet still lightly permeating the glass.

I dressed rather quickly, eager to enjoy my final day in Florence, and took the elevator down to find a motorbike with Leo on it. He grinned, "It's your last day here, would you like to see Florence from the perspective of a Florentine?" I laughed, "I would love to." He handed me a black helmet and I fastened it over my curls. The wind, turning unseasonably temperate with the tickle of sun, danced across my face as we puttered down the street. We drove past Santa Croce, then crossed a bridge over the Arno, zipping down various side alleys to the front of the Pitti Palace. Sitting at a table outside a café across from the Palace, we sipped espressos and watching groups of people amble by as rays of sunshine filtered through clouds in a Raphael-esque scene.

We ate a simple lunch of spinach salads with balsamic vinaigrette, shards of pecorino, and winter pears that burst open in an explosion of flavor. After lunch, Leo drove out into the countryside of Tuscany and we smoothly drove along the dirt roads, kicking up little sandstorms behind us. He turned off onto a side road and helped me off the bike to walk around a vineyard that a friend of his owned. Leo pointed out the parts of the grape vines, gently twirling strands of vine around his long fingers and resting his hands on the wooden poles that the vines strung along. He gently steered the bike back onto the highway. I touched the somewhat worn leather of the seat and tilted back my helmet-clad head to let the wind brush my face.

Just as I thought we were headed back to the city, Leo pulled off the road into a small village called Greve in Chianti. He led me down the deserted streets into a piazza facing a medieval church. Leo helped me up the stairs and tried to open the door to the *chiesa*, which supposedly held works by Fra Angelico. After knocking rather politely he laughed, "It is the time of afternoon rest, the schedule is not in our fortune today."

Leo and I made our way back to the city by twilight. We ate dinner at his favorite restaurant, a beautiful place with the slightest air of regret intermingled with the light trills of laughter from another table. A pianist played in the corner with the force of a maestro, his strength and passion flowing through his flying fingers. I listened to the piano, letting out a breath and almost laughing at the beauty and the way it pulled on my heartstrings. Chatting animatedly with the force of the piano behind us, I thanked Leo for showing me the undisturbed beauty of Tuscany. He smiled and lifted his water glass, toasting my safe return to America.

We finished our meal, chatting once more until Leo stood and walked over to the bar. He took a paper napkin and asked the bartender for a pen. Hovering over the table, he wrote down his email address and said, "For whenever you need a friend." I put the napkin in my purse. "*Ringrazio il mio amico*," I said and he laughed with pleasure at my snippet of Italian. We drove back to the Suites and he grinned, saying, "*Arrivederci* Nicolette, it was a true pleasure to meet you." I smiled and replied, "It was lovely to spend today with you, thank you." I waved goodbye as I plodded into the hotel, looked back to see Leo waving goodbye, and raised my hand.

After two hours of tossing and turning, I pulled my trench coat over my pajamas, and slipped into my shoes. I sat on the pavement of the Ponte Vecchio and listened to Claudio play his guitar, letting the music drift off into the night, carrying me with it.

The next morning, I rolled down the window ruefully as I drove to Milan, smelling the sweet air of the Italian countryside. I pulled up to the Hertz kiosk and, rather regretfully, handed over the keys to the car. I stepped into the airport and was caught in the whirlwind of travel and the rush of flying. The day passed, watching the tranquil ocean and powder clouds strewn across the horizon. When I arrived back in New York and finished going through immigration and customs, I spotted Amelia waiting for me, her children holding a welcome back sign, jollily decorated in fingerprints and bright paint.

As Amelia drove me home, my days in Florence seemed like a distant dream. A sense of dread and responsibility returned to me as I arrived back in the world I knew.

I was going to have a daughter to support – alone.

Chapter Three

The next morning, I traipsed to Zola, taking a deep breath as I entered the conference room for our monthly meeting to discuss new ideas for the company magazine, *The Ray*. I slid into one of the chairs around a polished teak table and sat up as my boss, April, jauntily stepped into the room.

As the meeting commenced, I heard April ask me what ideas I had. I smiled nervously and racked my brain, "While I had nothing prepared, I couldn't help but notice the fashions in Florence. They managed to make winter look stylish in the way that many American styles don't. We need a new take; we can revamp winter – Italian style." April jumped up from her chair, "Nicolette this is perfect, you are in charge of this article, send me ideas today; Jon – you design garments; Connor – put together color spreads; Marie – you're writing. Regina, you will be Nicolette's assistant."

Sitting back at my mahogany desk in a cushy chair, I unplugged my laptop and packed my bag, ready for my two-block walk home, excited about my new responsibility and upset that Aaron couldn't share my joy.

The end of January approached rapidly, my plethoric days filled with late nights, fabric samples, photos, and models. The clothes became a sensation around the office and Regina assisted me with the reality and challenges involved in the projects, making me ever more grateful for her experienced knowledge. We brimmed with anticipation for how the public would receive our hard work. My head ached with the flurried whirlwind of work and the strain on my body from my progressing pregnancy.

On a day when the winter's chill seemed to reach into my bones, lulling me out of the almost constant state of fatigue from my inundating work, I visited Aaron's grave with a bundle of bright red poppies. I knelt before the headstone, above where he lay, telling him tales of Italy and of my experiences since I had come home. I left, smiling sadly, thinking of what we should have had.

Although my life seemed to be moving forward, I could not shake a desire for something more. The numbness that had set in after Aaron's death seemed to reappear without warning. The woman who I was before Aaron's death and my pregnancy would have embraced this life, but I had changed. I sunk into my work with a restless fervor, trying to ward off the strong sadness that snuck up behind me, disconcerting me with its force.

I called Char, my twin brother's girlfriend and a friend of mine from college, on a day when the depression had greatened until I felt that the darkness had closed around me. Char arrived and I ran a self-conscious hand through my wildly curling hair, attempting to straighten a pile of stray articles and pictures on the kitchen counter that I had thus far shirked from editing. Char sauntered straight into the kitchen, her eyes shining with the clear sheen of a gem. As the comparison popped into my mind, I glimpsed the lustrous diamond on her ring finger. She squealed in her honeyed voice, "Mitch proposed! We're getting married as soon as possible, and I want you to be my bridesmaid!" She took in an abrupt gulp of air, and then looked at my face as it transformed with the bright smile of congratulations and happiness. After hugging her with excitement, she looked into my eyes and remarked, "Nicolette, you do not look okay," and then commanded, "Draw the water for a bath, pour some bubbles in, and I'll be right there to talk to you." She ordered me into the tub and disappeared as I slid into the tub, the bubbles multiplying and covering my rounded stomach.

I reclined into the suds, bubbles popping against my skin and the ends of my hair twirling around me, trailing in the water. Char calmly said, "Now tell me everything, no matter what it is, just tell me. You need to get it off your chest." I took a shuddery breath and started to cry, "Char, I don't want to be a burden to you, I just have no idea what's wrong with me. I'm depressed and I feel as if I'm trapped in some puppeteer's plan, some sort of dancing monkey at the whims of something bigger. I want to be in control of my life again. I can't handle this constant onslaught of work and pain and missing Aaron!" She listened, perched on the side of the bathtub and put a caring hand on my shoulder, "Nicolette, I think you need a break."

We sat there in silence, and mentally I left that day, remembering another cold day when Aaron still stood at my side. I had just returned home from a long day of modeling for a winter collections show, and sat on the edge of the tub in a fuzzy robe, my aching feet in the bath. My feet burned from the six-inch heels and I groaned as the powerful jets of water worked their way into my heels. Aaron snuck up behind me and kissed me on the lips. Sitting down next to me on the polished rim of the bath, he playfully splashed water onto me with his feet and I kicked back until we were splashing and spilling water like children, the pain in my feet long forgotten. He stopped kicking for a moment and put his arms around my terry cloth covered form and kissed me on the tip of my nose, "You know I love you more than anything, don't you?" I put my answer into a long, sweet kiss. My smile enveloped my face as he murmured, "How'd I ever get a girl like you?" He stroked my curls with his gentle hands and kissed me again, taking in every detail of my face as he kissed me across my strong jawline and up the curve of my cheek to my forehead. There he planted a kiss full of pure and simple love.

"Nicolette," murmured Char, breaking me from the reverie that left sudden tears streaming down my face and my heart ready to leap out of my chest. I could feel my lips throbbing as if Aaron had kissed me minutes ago, not months. I put a smile on my face and thanked Char before shooing her out of the room as I stepped out of the bathtub, my heart full of emotion and belly feeling even heavier a weight than before. I sunk into a half-awake, half-asleep state and waited for the blaring of my alarm to shake me into consciousness.

After a long day of working and negotiating with my colleagues over the spreads for the magazine, I sunk down into the desk chair in my office and put a weary hand over where my baby kicked. I let out the breath that I had been holding in and shut my eyes. Connor, a colleague and old friend, found me in my office with my head in my hands as I tried to ward off the stealthily approaching migraine. He unquestioningly hugged me. I realized how much I needed human closeness and put my face into his shoulder. He let go of me for a moment and looked into my eyes, saying, "It's not as bad as it seems; it never is. Life has its lows and highs and you will pass through them all with grace." I gave him a half smile and thanked him as he took my hand and squeezed it.

Connor helped me to pack my bag, picked up my various folders, and escorted me to the lobby. We stood in silence as the elevator descended to the ground floor. Connor looked at my tired face and hands, jittery from sheer exhaustion, and told me, "Nicolette, I'm going to walk you home, you don't look well." He motioned for me to give him my bag and took my arm. Slowly, we walked down the street, our pale reflections mirrored in the sheen of the buildings, ghostly halos of streetlights silhouetting the barren trees, sleet dribbling through naked branches. We maneuvered our way to my building and after we took the elevator up to my condo, he helped me inside.

Connor kissed me on the forehead, took my hand, told me to rest, and left. I lowered my aching body onto a chair in the kitchen, spine curved forward in fatigue. I realized that the things I used to care most about no longer seemed to matter. I pulled on fleecy pajamas and sank onto my bed putting my head to my knees and pondering my life. Why would God do this to me? My husband was gone, I was pregnant alone, and as much as I loved my job, it was dragging me down into stress and tension. I picked up the phone and dialed my mother, the one person I could always speak freely to. She answered the phone and greeted me cheerfully. I responded trying to pull myself back together when suddenly I fell apart. My ever-so-calmly composed exterior crumbled into tears, "I'm sorry Mom, I don't know what's wrong with me." Her soft voice murmured calming words that I didn't quite hear and she said that she was on her way to my condo to see me. I heard a light tapping on my door and opened it to let my mother in. She wrapped her thin arms around me and I bent down to hug her.

She took my hand as we sat down on the couch, wrapped in silence for a moment. Her voice seemed to echo, "Oh my Nicolette, you were always such a happy girl. It is the most terrible thing in the world when the worst things happen to special people." "I can't seem to bring myself to do any of the things I used to love. Everything here reminds me of Aaron." I leaned backward into the cushions of the couch, my body caving into the plushness. The exhaustion of the work and the sadness and the responsibility that came with Aaron's death and our baby seemed to pile more and more upon my already heavy load. For the second time in twenty-four hours, I had succumbed to my sadness and I felt weaker for it. "Nicolette, I promise you, it is not a weakness to show fear and sadness; it is a strength. Allowing yourself to really feel your sadness is a step towards healing and happiness, towards that sunrise after a sleepless night." I squeezed her hand and tilted my head onto her shoulder and whispered, "Thank you. For everything." She ran her soft hand through my hair like she had when I was just a child and I ran my hand over where my baby stirred. "This baby is a gift," I thought, "This is our life and we have to live it to the fullest."

My eyes slid shut with the thought and I felt my mother gently holding me. "Thank you for being here for me Mom." She reached up and stroked my face with a tender hand, "I will always be here for you, Nicolette. Goodnight darling."

Chapter Four

The next morning, I emailed April that I was ill and would not be at work that day. Body worn into the concave of the bed, I shivered with the restlessness that carried me back to sleep. I woke up mid-morning from a vivid dream in which I sat in the Palazzo Vecchio, a soft pencil rolling on the chilled marble next to me. David stood, staring at me and reached out his hand in a gesture that seemed to say, "Come child." I stepped towards him and the dream disappeared as I sat up abruptly in bed. The sun flickered drowsily through transparent blinds and nostalgia washed over me. Crossing my legs and putting my chin in my hands, I wondered what I was going to do next. I felt like I barely had a life in New York anymore and sighed as I thought back on the magnificence of the Arno's stationary frozen surface and the calming buttery yellow tones of the Ponte Vecchio. My mind flooded with the images of Florence until they exploded into a flare of light, holding a single question, "What if I moved to Florence?" The sparks of my memories fizzled in the after-light of the detonation. My eyes began to glimmer with the possibilities. I could create a new life for my daughter; I could start over and find my dreams and passions again. I had lost track of my purpose during those days of loss and mourning, I had to discover and feel life again. Finally understanding what I wanted, I climbed out of bed and got to work immediately searching for apartments to rent in Florence.

That afternoon, I walked to my mom's office and knocked on her door to find her sitting behind a pile of folders and papers. "Hello Nicolette!" she exclaimed. I responded with matched enthusiasm and rushed to kiss her on the cheek. "Well you're sounding much better," she smiled. I sat next to her and took a deep breath, "Mom, I think I found my way out." She looked puzzled for a second, thinking about our conversation. I spoke up again, "I'm going to leave New York. I have been thinking about Florence ever since I left. I don't think about Aaron's death every other second there – rather, I can envision him alive and well. Our daughter will have a new start there. I have been looking at apartments and I think that I can find a reasonably priced one. Will you support me in doing this?" Her eyes searched mine as a slow smile spread across her face, "I think that you will be happy there because I know that you will be happy anywhere. You need a new start and if this is what you want to do, of course I support you. I couldn't be more proud of you." I wrapped my arms around her gratefully. She piped up again, "And do expect some house guests, your father and I have always wanted to spend a few months in Florence." I laughed and promised her that she would be welcome any time. We talked details for over an hour before I hugged her one more time and stepped out of her office, my heart feeling lighter than it had in months.

The next day, I returned to work with purpose and knocked on the door to April's office. Her voice resonated, laughing, and I peeked into the room. April murmured, "I'll see you tonight," and hung up. She looked at me kindly, "Are you feeling better?" I took a deep breath and responded calmly, "Yes, thank you. April, I have loved working here and it has been an honor being a member of your team. This last assignment has been absolutely amazing and I appreciate the confidence you have placed in me, but I can no longer see a life for my daughter and myself here in New York. We are going to start anew in Italy." April sat up straight, surprised, then nodded, "Nicolette, I understand that you've been through a lot, but are you sure that you want to make any large life changes right now?" After a pause I said, "This is what I want. I will finish *The Ray*'s Winter Issue and if you would like, I can freelance write from Italy on their trends. I will wrap up everything that I am in charge of here and finish the Winter Issue in the next two weeks. My baby and I need a new start and I want to spend as much time with her as possible." She sighed and asked, "Is there anything that I can say to convince you otherwise?" I simply shook my head. April told me that I would get a final paycheck for two months and a bonus for all of my work on the magazine. She then added that she would love for me to freelance from Florence writing a column per issue and I would be paid accordingly. I thanked her and left her office to arrange my leave.

In between setting my departure in order, I searched for an apartment, emailing back and forth with friendly Florentines. Rather quickly, I discovered a charming apartment on the fifth floor of a building on the edge of the Arno. I called Amelia to tell her about my decisions and my future. Her first response was, "You quit your job – what are you thinking?" After her outburst, Amelia argued that I was simply having a crisis due to the state my life was in. I disagreed, patiently, as I told her that I had the support of Mom and Dad already and that it was what I needed for a new start. She said that she and I were going to spend Saturday together and in an indignant undertone stated that someone needed to talk sense into me. I laughed at the fact that she thought she could change my mind as I began to hum, dreaming about raising an Italian daughter in that beautiful Tuscan city.

I went to work each day with renewed verve, my new beginning approaching with every minute. I planned my column with April, promising to deliver one every other month. Slowly, my vision for my new life became clearer.

That weekend, Amelia arrived to find me happily humming and tidying up the house in yoga pants and a t-shirt with my hair twisted up in a bun. She hugged me and asked me how I was feeling. Then she got down to business, "Ok, now," she said in a no nonsense voice, "What are you doing? Deciding to move to Italy on a lark just because of a few days there? God, we never should have bought you that ticket!"

She took a deep breath and asked, "Nicolette, why are you doing this? Your family is here, why would you move half a world away?" I looked into her eyes, the same shape as the ones I looked out of every day, and said, "Amelia, I cannot continue to live a life in New York where I constantly see places that Aaron and I planned to go or went and where I ask, "What if?" every minute. This is my one fleeting life and I have to live it." Her eyes opened wide in surprise and she nodded slowly, "You're actually happy ... and if this makes you feel good, then I guess you should do it - but I'm going to help you. You are past five months pregnant, you should not be dealing with this by yourself." She took my hand, asking me to tell her my plans. I told her that I planned to rent out my condo as it would be a steady source of income because Aaron and I had paid off the mortgage and it was fairly spacious and fully furnished. Amelia listened and then asked what other money I had, because my Italian stay might last longer than either of us expected. I responded that I had the money Aaron had left me, Aaron's life insurance, and much of the money that I earned in my years as a model and fashion designer. I would also be freelance writing for Zola on Italian fashion – if that was not enough, I could go back to work as a model after my daughter was born or I could find another job.

Amelia and I created an ad to post online that advertised a fully furnished, two bedroom, one-and-a-half bathroom condo for $3,500 a month. We posted pictures of it along with my phone number and e-mail address at the bottom. Within a few days, I had received six calls and eight e-mails. We invited all of them to visit the condo over the course of two days. All of the potential renters sent me e-mails saying how much they would offer. When the highest bidders both offered $3,800, I told them that whoever was willing to pay $4,000 per month would be able to rent the condo in my absence.

I called my lawyer and she wrote up the lease to send to the family that was willing to pay my requested rent. It turned out to be a wealthy older couple that was moving back into the city after a grand European tour and wanted a nice place to stay put for a little while. They agreed to pay me on the fourteenth of each month and if I was not back in one year, they could sign an extension on the lease. They would move in at the end of the month and I would leave for Italy the evening they moved in.

The process of planning my move to Florence was quick and easy and the apartment there boasted a beautiful open plan living area with a gorgeous view. It had just enough furniture for comfort but not too much to make it cluttered. I started to donate some of Aaron's clothes to local charities and moved paintings, my books, and a piece or two of our best furniture into a storage unit. I began packing my clothes into boxes and included the baby blankets and clothes I had bought over the past months. Grateful for the E.U. Passport that I had thanks to my French-born mother, I was able to arrange the paperwork quickly. With only two suitcases and six boxes, I was ready to start my new life.

Near the end of February, our closest friends and family attended the rehearsal dinner for Char and Mitch's wedding. In a quiet moment, Mitch took me aside, "Sis, I'm so proud of you. I know you're doing the right thing." A smile spread across my face and I hugged him, "Thank you Mitch, you and Char are going to have a wonderful life together." The rest of the party was a blurry haze, filled with laughing and toasting, and a few hours later we all left with the promise of seeing each other one more time at Mitch and Char's wedding.

The next morning flooded the Earth with light, dancing off of the buildings and playfully peeking into the windows. On my way to the wedding, I thought for a moment on the major stages of life: birth, marriage, and death. By July, we would have had one of each: Aaron's death, Char and Mitch's wedding, and my daughter's birth.

The wedding was beautiful; Char strolled down the aisle, radiant in a Vera Wang dress that clung to her chest and fell in a cascade of silk at her hips, swirling past her feet into a train that one of Amelia's daughters carried proudly. A diamond tiara secured the long white veil that muffled the grin enveloping Char's face. Her hair curled down past her shoulders, entwined with complicated braids. Mitch seemed simply astounded to see the woman he loved meeting him at the altar. My mother sat in a pew, sighing and crying simultaneously as my father clutched her hand with a reminiscent smile upon his face. Joy filled the chapel, the air clouded with its sweetness and simplicity.

The guests flooded out of the church's worn doors, ebulliently awaiting the appearance of the newlyweds. Our hands flew into the air, scattering grains of rice to the wind as Char and Mitch held hands, tripping giddily down the stairs in their blissfully shared state. As they tumbled toward the car, Char threw her bouquet back to the women of the wedding. Laughing, we reached up for it, truly not minding who would catch it. Char looked back once more and winked as the bouquet landed in my arms.

The reception was full of friends and family and the room burst with chatter and laughter. When all of the guests had finished eating, we flooded onto the dance floor. The music started to play and Connor came over to me and jokingly bowed as he pulled me up from my chair. We laughingly rocked back and forth to the music, ducking and spinning as we went. On slower songs, he and I swayed to the gentle waves of music. Finally, when my legs were aching and my throat was dry from talking and laughing, I hugged Connor, said goodbye, and walked towards where Amelia was sitting chatting to one of her friends. Seeing the happy yet exhausted look on my face, she smiled, tread over to me, and asked, "Are you ready to go home?" I quietly nodded, "That would be amazing, thank you for being so good to me." She answered with a hug.

I reached my last day at work, feeling slightly rueful. I said goodbye to everyone, receiving many tearful hugs. April told me that I had been a good colleague and that if I ever needed a full time job again, I should call her. Connor helped me take my boxes down to a taxi. As we stood beside the cab, the driver waiting for me to get in, Connor kissed my cheek and gave me a hug, and said, "I'll miss you Nicolette." I squeezed his hand and replied, "I'll miss you too Connor, you're a true friend. I hope that you are very successful." Hand fluttering in the air in goodbye, I looked once more at the glint of the building where I had expected to work for many years to come.

On the day before my new life began, Char, Mitch, Mom, Dad, and Amelia came to my condo and gave me a few final presents for the baby and said their last goodbyes. Mom bit her lip and let a tear drip past her lashes as she made me promise to email, text, and Skype her often. I squeezed her hand and promised that I'd call her and be with her in spirit always, just like before, and that there would always be room for her in my apartment. I gave Char a tight hug, wishing her the best time on her honeymoon. She grinned but also held a sad look in her eyes as she said, "I can't believe you're going to be this far away." I grinned back at her, "You and Mitch have a life to start!" Mitch hugged me as I brought his bride back to him. All of them promised to visit after the baby was born. We parted, bittersweet smiles on our faces, waving goodbye. I stood in front of the building for a few minutes after they left, feeling like Scarlett O'Hara out of *Gone With the Wind* with my long autumn colored skirt billowing around me and dark tendrils of hair whipping across my face.

I bade farewell to my home, handing the renters the key and catching a cab to the airport. My hands shook with excitement and anticipation. The cab driver noticed my anxiousness and laughed, a low and throaty sound, saying with a rich African accent, "You have the nerves?" I nodded, my nervous energy flooding through the car. With a voice that shook up and down like a beginner pianist's scales, I said, "I'm leaving everything I know for a new life and trying to escape reality by chasing after a few fleeting moments of happiness." He smiled in a worldly way and his voice echoed thorough the car, "Well Missus I did just that when I was young like you and came here to America," He paused proudly and continued, "and let me just say, I am as happy as can be to call this country home. Chase that happiness you're seeking and find it." He smiled again and I realized that wisdom is spread far and wide and granted to a lucky few, and this taxi driver knew more about finding joy than many of the most educated scholars. He was silent the rest of the way, but when we got to the airport, he gave me one last morsel of advice, "Never, ever give up on chasing your dreams. What may have seemed like the most harebrained, crazy idea can always have a fairy tale ending."

I strode light-headedly towards the flight that would lead me to Florence; my heart tap-danced in my chest as I took small, quick steps in my black boots. As I boarded the plane, my breath came in little spurts and the flight passed quickly in sleep. I awoke and watched in awe as dawn smeared her paints across the sky, tingeing mountains pink and shadowing the plains with a blue mist. The patchwork assembly of Europe stitched itself into a flowing quilt below me. Gravity pulled the plane into the midst of the meandering rivers and sun-enveloped land and the plane touched down with a jolt. I ambled off the plane with one hand on my stomach and the other clinging to my purse.

And in that moment, so insignificant in the history of the world, I stepped into my future.

DAWN

Chapter Five

I slid exhaustedly into a cab with my suitcases and purse and directed the driver to my new apartment. When I arrived at the front door, the owner of the apartment, Paola, stood waiting with a bright smile. She showed me to where my boxes were and offered to drop by the next day to help me. I accepted with a hearty nod and she kissed me on each cheek, wished me a good rest, and left. I rested in the chair in my bedroom aside a draped window. Then, in the direction of my belly, I whispered, "For you, I will do anything. This will be a grand adventure for the two of us, won't it?" I sighed quietly, "Oh Aaron, if only you were here." My voice trailed off into the silence of the room and I dressed myself in a warm pair of pajamas. Sleep greeted me, screaming out the haunting doubts that I warded off so carefully during the reign of day. In the dark of night, these thoughts danced through my head in a terrifying tango and taunted me with the puckered snarls that snagged the fabric of my life.

I woke up, with a blanket I had carelessly thrown over myself the night before tangled around my limbs and my forehead covered in a sheen of sweat, to a thump on my door. I pulled myself out of bed and padded over to the door to find Paola there, dressed in a t-shirt and jeans, ready to help me with my boxes.

I stepped over to her, stretching out my aching back. First, we unpacked my sewing machine and fabrics and she showed me a cabinet with the perfect amount of space for the fabric bolts on the bottom and the machine on the top. In the room that would be the baby's, we unpacked clothes into a chest of drawers and I organized her toys onto a shelf. Paola helped me attach a mobile to the ceiling and then we moved onto my room. She and I made up the bed with proper sheets, then she helped me hang up some of Aaron's paintings and some of mine around the apartment. In my bedroom she gave me converters for my various electronics. The six boxes were unpacked one by one until the apartment looked like it belonged to me. Then, after everything was unpacked, she said she had something to give me and that she would be right back.

She reappeared pushing a large item on wheels covered with a sheet. She nodded and I lifted the sheet. Underneath lay the most beautiful crib I had ever seen. It was dark polished wood with carvings of flowers lining the sides. My eyes welled with tears and I stammered out a thank you. We moved it into the baby's room and I asked her a question I had been dying to ask, "Might I paint the walls of this room for her?" I watched her as I saw her mouth form the word 'sí.'

Fit to do nothing more, I simply pulled on my pajamas and lay down on the plush bed. I drifted off to sleep and the pleasant opposite of the previous night's dreams swept through my head: a beautiful baby, Aaron, and I sat together on the banks of the Arno, the wind whispering sweet songs around us and the water lapping at our feet. My head rested in Aaron's lap and he sat stroking my hair. The baby slept peacefully in my arms. We stayed like that for the longest time until I could almost feel the sun warming my skin and Aaron's gentle hands running through my hair. The baby stirred in my arms and her eyes fluttered open, revealing Aaron's bright eyes. I woke up with tears wet on my face. Knowing that I could not sit in sadness the whole day, I decided to go out and explore my new town.

I dressed quickly, throwing my trench coat over my shoulders and putting on a pair of smoky-colored gloves. Then realizing that I had barely eaten dinner the previous night, I wandered off in search of a Nutella waffle. When that mission was complete, I inhaled the waffle and continued my stroll. I found the indoor food market that I had gone to with my cooking class and bought fabulously frivolous foods. I purchased fresh *mozzarella di bufala* and juicy tomatoes, bursting with freshness and flavor. Persimmons to prosecco and vinegar to virgin olive oil, I bought it all.

I struggled home with two bags threatening to overflow and stacked them into the empty fridge that beckoned to the foods with cool arms. A hollow knock sounded on the front door and I strode over to open it, untying my coat and throwing it over a barstool as I went. The door swung open and revealed a pretty, petite Italian woman. She gave me a big smile and started babbling in rapid Italian. I grinned and put my hand up for a moment before saying, "Hello! I'm sorry, I don't speak Italian very well." She laughed and easily switched to English, saying, "Welcome, my name is Marina. I am your neighbor from down the hall! What is your name?" I giggled as two little boys and a little girl shyly poked their faces out from behind her skirt. "My name is Nicolette, I just moved here from New York," I said. Marina grinned and beckoned her little girl forward. The child was holding a tin foil covered dish and Marina smiled saying, "It is for you to eat and enjoy! You need good food for the child." I laughed and thanked her as she introduced her children, "This one is Marco, he is five and the very devil he is! This is Gian; he is six. And this is my baby, Bella, she is three." She beamed with motherly pride as her children stepped forward, one by one. After that, Marina said goodbye, promising to visit and bring friends to meet soon. I grinned, knowing that I had a new friend in Florence.

I opened the foil-covered dish to discover a pastry created with chocolate, gelato, and an Italian biscotti bottom. Unable to stop myself, I found a spoon that I had unpacked the day before and dug in not bothering to dish an amount onto a plate. In almost no time, half of the treat was gone and I laughed at my lack of self-restraint. I went to bed and let sleep fall upon me, not caring if dreams visited or not.

I rose late to the chirps and caws of birds and ventured into the bathroom to arrange my beauty products and perfumes on the pale wooden shelves. Next, I hung my clothes carefully, trying to hold back the flood of memories accompanying each one. A huge bathtub stood proudly, held up by old-fashioned golden colored paws, next to a window that looked onto the Arno with soft golden curtains drawn around it. I fell more in love with my new home with each passing moment.

I dressed in warm clothes and trekked out into the streets just in time to see perfect Italian flakes of snow falling from the sky. I concealed a childlike giggle at the frivolity and happiness of pure snow and ambled to the café where I had been on my first visit. I ordered the same delicious white hot chocolate and a *biscotto* to nibble on. I sat contemplatively, as if I was living in someone else's life, perched in front of the fire long after I had finished my food and drink. I ambled out of the café and into the snowy streets. The piles of snow were rapidly growing as the number of floating flakes grew. I let go of all rigidity and formality and spun in a little circle, letting my hair float out around me and not caring who saw.

The next week passed in a blur of new friends coming and going, visiting the same café again and again, and sketching in different squares and museums. I rediscovered my love of art with a burning passion, drawing whatever I could from my own hands to the view from my window to the plethora of statues to the rich architectural treasures. I thanked God for the English news magazine in Florence, *The Florentine*, because my Italian, although improving, remained tentative. I found events, book recommendations, and restaurants to visit within its well-informed pages.

March arrived and I went to Marina's Ob/Gyn, Doctor Niccolo. He kindly welcomed me into the hospital and showed me around, gently asking questions and getting to know me. He put me at ease with his tender manner and I quickly grew to trust him. I went on two visits to the hospital to meet the other doctors, learn the procedures, and visit the birthing wing.

I rested as my new doctor advised me to and spent many leisurely days relaxing, trying out recipes in my compact kitchen, and working on paintings of the view out of my window. I appreciated Marina's friendship, support, and sense of humor. She visited me with her children, who every time became less shy. They crawled into my lap and cuddled with me, touching my belly and looking inquisitively at me. They began to call me Zia Nicolette and I loved spending precious hours with them. Marina taught me recipes and visited every day with fresh ingredients for us to cook with. Every recipe was a revelation, and Marina the angel conducting the heavenly choirs that sang as I bit into the scrumptious food.

I explored Florence, wanting to get to know every cobblestone on the ground and every brick of each building. Each day, I felt more like Alice when she fell down the rabbit hole, awed by the almost magical beauty of everything. Going a little further each day, I savored each moment that I spent on the streets. When I became exhausted, I would go back to my apartment to cook or stop at a sidewalk café for a nibble. I discovered many little restaurants during my ambulatory adventures and each had something special hidden within it: a stunning painting by an unknown artist, a bit of crumbled architecture in the basement from Roman days, or a divine pasta recipe, handed down through generations and cooked with love. At night, I went out onto the Ponte Vecchio and watched Claudio, the guitarist, or another musician depending on the night.

Chapter Six

A sense of peace that I had forgotten settled over me and I accepted its gentle haze. The Italian breezes cleared my head and let me think about the life I had known and how it was about to change even more drastically. On the nights that I lay in bed past midnight pondering life, my thoughts fell on Aaron often and I missed him so very much. I could see him smiling, laughing, kissing me, dancing with me, and sleeping – his peace radiating from within. His eyes haunted my nightmares and danced in my dreams. Our daughter's kicks grew stronger and the thought that there was a small person inside me who was part of Aaron and me delighted me beyond measure.

March dragged along in a pleasant fashion and spring slowly arrived in Florence, a drape of pink shrouding her slender shoulders and a warm grin spreading across her pale face. The littlest things made me smile – even the sound of a recycling truck early in the morning or a Vespa speeding by late at night when I tried to sleep. I walked through the streets, looking at the windows of stores where mannequins peeked out, leaning forward, as if to whisper a secret. I wrote my first column for *The Ray* about the coming spring days and the filmy long skirts and light trench coats that accompanied the sun.

I painted my baby's room over the course of two days. I began with a slender cherry blossom tree in full bloom at sunrise. I painted little blossoms flying in an unseen breeze into the Italian countryside in the brightness of day: rolling hills, twisting rivers, twirling grape vines, and dancing Cyprus trees – the walls melting into one another.

As I reached up with my paintbrush to put the finishing touches to a cloud, a hollow knock sounded on my door. "Come in!" I dabbed a splotch of paint over the spot and heaved a deep breath as I sat down on a stool, smiling at the walls around me. Marina pranced in, the shadow of a man following behind her. "Nicolette," she laughed hugging me, "This is my brother, Leo. I was telling him about you moving in and he thought he might know you." I grinned, "Leo, hello!" He smiled and kissed me on either cheek, "Nicolette, how are you?" We moved into the kitchen and I filled the espresso pot. The three of us sat talking long into the evening about their childhood and my decision to move to Italy. We laughed and talked – both of them detailing excitedly how they had figured out that Leo knew me. As night fell, they left, grinning, and promising to visit me again.

One day, I discovered a puppet shop with hand-painted marionettes. Their gaudy colors shone through the rainy day as if a ray of sunshine had fallen into that shop. I bought a girl in a vibrant violet dress that reminded me of the Heidi stories I had read as a young girl and placed her on a shelf in my daughter's room.

As I visited the many churches that Florence had to offer, I found myself unknowingly adding God into my daily life again. I forgave Him for taking Aaron and as that bitterness slipped away, I felt a small freedom.

One day, the baby's kicks became more urgent and painful. Worried, I sought my doctor. Doctor Niccolo's eyes betrayed slight worry as I told him my symptoms, but took on a reassuring look as he told me that my body did not want to carry to term. He prescribed full bed rest until my due date. I tried to take deep breaths on the cab ride home, warding away the fear that smothered me from within. With each breath a word, "She will be okay, she has to be okay."

In my sleep that night, I dreamed of a child, her eyes open in a glassy stare, dead. Looking closer, I saw myself next to the babe, lifeless also. A haunted voice accused me for the baby's death, for Aaron's death, for my own death. The dream began to swirl into shadows and my doubts chased me, nipping at my ankles. I could no longer run and they grabbed my legs, pulling me into their darkness.

My breath was ragged as I awoke and I felt like I had run a marathon. The solemn darkness of pre-dawn surrounded the apartment and I turned on a light, waiting for the safety of day to drag me away from my thoughts. I tried to read, but unable to make out the words, stopped. I closed my eyes and tried to remember a memory when Aaron was with me.

My thoughts fell onto our first dance.

~ Middle school – my first real dance. The DJ just announced that it was the last dance of the night; I had declined every invitation to dance from other boys with the hope that Aaron would ask. I turned around to see him standing there. "Nicolette, will you dance with me?" asked that shy but sure voice I knew so well. "I'd love to," I replied, trying fiercely to keep the giddiness I felt out of my voice. He placed his hands gently on my waist. We swayed to the song and our friends cried out, "Ooooh, it's lo-ove," making hearts with their hands and holding them up to us. As the song progressed, I became braver, sliding my hands around his neck. His hands slid around my waist and landed on the small of my back. I rested my head against his chest, he hugged me closer and I could feel his breath against the side of my face; a song had never lasted longer than those first moments in each other's arms. ~

The reverie only made me miss him more. At six o' clock, the garbage truck rumbled by my window and jolted me to a slightly more awake state. Glass crushed into the cans and each crash of the shattering bottles jolted me upwards. The hour slowly passed and finally, around seven, I got out of bed and went to take a bath. I lit several vanilla scented candles and poured aromatic, peppermint oils into the hot water. The swirls made little patterns similar to the sky in Van Gogh's tortured

Starry Night. I slipped down until the water shrouded my neck and closed my eyes as I let the water release the tension in my shoulders and back.

As I made breakfast, the sound of a knock and Marina's voice echoed through the apartment. I opened the door and Marina came in inquiring happily how I was. I told her in my improving Italian that I had to be at rest until the baby was born. She took my hand and we walked into my room. She opened the blinds and let the bright sunlight flood in and course through the room. I sunk onto a pillow-padded armchair while Marina braided my hair just as she braided Bella, her daughter's. She pulled up a chair next to mine and brought me a glass of milk. I curled up with my feet beneath me, sipping slowly from the glass as Marina and I discussed what I should be doing to best keep myself and my baby healthy until the due date. As my eyes drooped shut, Marina wrapped an arm around me and led me to my bed, tucking me in and with fretting hands, arranged the blankets. She stacked a pile of books from my bookshelf next to me and told me to rest, assured me she would visit later, and left.

Later, as I leant against a pile of pillows, reading tranquilly, the door swung open and Leo walked in, "Nicolette, Marina told me you were not so well." He pulled up a chair next to my bed and asked what I was reading. He stayed and talked and returned every few days with a meal or a new book or magazine. My mother, father, Amelia, Char and Mitch were my virtual companions over Skype.

So the hours of rest passed, the pile of books to read growing smaller, the pages of my sketchbook fuller, the visits from Leo and Marina longer, and the kicks from the baby stronger. The rest strengthened me, my worries and tensions dissipating with the soft release of withdrawal from the world.

On the easier days, Marina and I would sit together in the armchairs in my room, breathing in the crisp spring air that pulsated through the room from open windows, the song of Florence booming and my heart lifted in it. On the more difficult days, I rested, sleep hard to greet and painful consciousness unthinkable – on those days, Leo and Marina would stay a little longer. As I flipped through my novels and baby books, I scribbled names on a flimsy slip of paper, narrowing the choices of my baby's name to Arianna, Alba, Aria, and Aurora, all starting with the same letter as Aaron.

Chapter Seven

On the third of April – the day that would have been Aaron's birthday – I sat at the kitchen counter, head in hands, arms bared against the cold marble. My womb cramped and tightened. I dismissed it, tears running down my face, sunken in disbelief that Aaron would never celebrate his twenty-eighth birthday. I wiped my eyes, pressing away the tears. My womb contracted; I doubled over in pain and struggled to stand. Marina strolled in about ten minutes later and my womb contracted again as the door flung open. In slow sentences, interrupted by my heavy breathing, I told Marina what was happening. Her face changed; she informed me that we were going to the hospital immediately. She hurried into my room and snatched my hospital bag from the closet, then told me to sit on a chair by the door to the apartment. She called her husband and he carried me down the stairs to her car, my body jolted with each step and head aching with the pound of fresh air and glare of sun. The contractions grew worse and I began to take sharp, quick intakes of breath, almost panting. My mind ran rampant, afraid, I thought, "Oh God, oh God, help me."

Marina flicked her eyes back and forth from the road to me, hands clenched upon the steering wheel. Arriving at the hospital, Marina rushed me to the desk, supporting me with her arm. She instructed in Italian that they had to see me immediately. They quickly took me up to a room; my contractions were occurring every four minutes. They dressed me in a hospital gown as I prayed that the baby was okay. With another fierce contraction, the world disappeared into darkness.

I floated between consciousness and the dusky world I had been pulled into. I could hear my cries and registered pain. Suddenly my cries disappeared and I heard frenzied voices and beeping in the outside world. I stood, my arms wrapped around Aaron. A soft haze surrounded us with the pale halo of a black and white photograph. He held me tight, his eyes closed, tears coursing down his cheeks. His eyes opened and I stared into their blue depths – the last glance that we never had. I choked back a sob. His voice echoed in my ears, "This is it Nicolette. You can either stay here with me or go to her," his voice quivered, "I beg you not to leave her – our baby will need you. But it is your choice and no matter what you choose, I love you – more than anything, for always." He hugged me close and his voice broke as he repeated, "I love you. I love you. I love you." I buried my head in his chest and luxuriated in a warmth that felt so real. Our lips met and I whispered, "I love you, I always will."

Fevered spasms tore through me. My eyes opened to see the doctor holding up a tiny baby girl as I set Aaron free to the life beyond this one. I breathed a final shivering sob. Our baby's cry pierced the room. My chest rose up and down, ragged breaths escaping. The doctor handed my baby to me.

I thought I had known joy before that day, but as my baby was placed in my arms, a new warm, tingling, emotion alive with light and love washed over me in buckets, the true meaning of the word, "joy," flooding my mind. I cradled her and whispered in her tiny ear, "I love you, you are my world." She gave a little coo and snuggled against me. The doctor took her out of my arms and I reluctantly released her, knowing that I would hold her again soon. Marina rushed to my side, crying, saying that I had stopped breathing, "Thank God, oh Nicolette!" My breathing steadied with my head rested on her shoulder, my body loosening and my heart slowing from its staccato beat. Marina touched my head and pressed her fingers in the outline of a cross on my forehead. I hugged her again and she hurried into the hallway, phone pressed to her ear. I closed my eyes, the darkness filled with Aaron and the wish that he could be there to see his baby. My mind ran through our goodbye, wrapping itself around every detail, every motion, every word. His warmth still flooded over me, promising our daughter and me the chance to live the life he would never have.

The moment that my baby was placed back in my arms, I held her close to me. The doctor assured me that while she was small, she was perfect in every way; she would be a healthy baby. I soaked up the feeling of finally holding the baby that I had carried for what seemed a small eternity. I cradled her, listening to her soft breath, stroking her tiny dimpled hand. Her eyes gazed intently into mine.

I realized with a whisper of a sob that she had Aaron's eyes. Her hair was dark and soft like mine, and her little lips curved into a pale red 'm.' A fuzzy pink blanket swaddled her body and her face peeked out of the folds and creases of the rosy cloth. My list of names spun through my head and as I examined her pale face and rose blossom cheeks, I decided on the name Alba. Alba means dawn in Italian. My daughter was my *alba*, my dawn – the dawn that woke me from the night that had carried me from Aaron. Alba pulled me closer to the sunrise that I was waiting for and drew the tips of the sun's rays into my life. Her middle name would be Joy because that is what she brought. Alba Joy Caulders, Aaron Joseph Caulders – they shared the same initials.

Cradled in my arms, Alba had fallen asleep, and I joined her in its refuge. I felt a hand on top of mine and my eyes flew open. Leo peered down at Alba, a soft grin spread across his face, "Marina told me that you'd had your baby. She's beautiful." "Thank you," I murmured, my eyes light, "her name is Alba Joy." He touched her head lightly, "*Buongiorno* Alba

Joy." I smiled softly and without realizing it, drifted back to sleep with my baby in my arms.

I awoke to the feeling of Alba squirming and opening her mouth hungrily. Marina dozed in a chair, face soft in peace; Leo paced in the hallway, vividly gesturing as he talked on the phone, a smile vibrant on his lips. Alba lay awake in my arms, looking up at me. My heart felt as if it were about to burst with the love I felt for my daughter.

After nursing Alba with instructions and help from the nurse, I saw Leo sitting in the hallway and called him in. Marina stirred and pulled her chair up to the bed. The three of us sat, chatting quietly. Marina took Alba out of my arms, gently rocking her back and forth and murmuring an Italian lullaby. I asked Leo if he wanted to hold her; looking a little frightened, he agreed and took her in his arms. Marina calmly doled instructions as he swayed softly.

I asked Marina to find my computer at the apartment so that I could tell my family that Alba had been born and introduce her live over Skype. When Marina returned with my laptop, I dialed my mom, who would be just arriving at work. She answered with a grin and asked how I was. Then looking at my surroundings, her expression morphed into concern, "Nicolette where are you? Are you all right?" I said simply, "Mama, everything is perfect, I had the baby early." I heard a sharp intake of breath as she quietly exclaimed, "You had the baby? Are you both alright?" I smiled softly, "We're perfect." Her voice was worried, "Oh thank God." I adjusted the computer so that she could see Alba, who was sleeping in my arms, "Meet Alba Joy." My mom's eyes watered and she whispered in a voice of awe, "She's beautiful. She's so little." My eyes teared up, "I wish you were here with me, I wish you could hold her. She is a miracle." In that moment, my mom's watering eyes flooded and turned into full out sobs, uttering, "I wish I was there Nicolette, you're my baby too." I smiled through the film of tears. She promised to come in a few days so that she could help me take care of Alba. After talking a little while longer, we hung up, red faced and smiling.

I wiped the stains of my tears from my face and after a few minutes, Skyped Stacy, Aaron's mother. She answered and greeted me cheerfully. I wasted no time in saying, "Stacy, I want to introduce you to your granddaughter." Her mouth dropped open and she stammered, "But she wasn't due until May." I shook my head and replied that she had come early. I held Alba higher up and closer to me so that Stacy could see her, "Meet Alba Joy Caulders." Her reaction was similar to my mother's and she called John over from the next room to see his granddaughter. "She has the same birthday as Aaron," I murmured. Smiling, with sad eyes, they promised to come to visit Alba and me soon and hung up.

I stayed in the hospital for three more days while they did tests on Alba to make sure that she was breathing well, verified that I was okay after my rough pregnancy and Alba's troubling birth, and assured that Alba was nursing properly. Leo and Marina appeared regularly to check on us and make sure that I was not lonely.

I took careful steps out of the hospital, holding Alba close to me. I gingerly stepped out to Marina's car and strapped Alba into a car seat, ducking in to sit next to her. Marina and Leo helped me up to my apartment and moved the crib into my bedroom.

After nursing Alba, I rested her softly in her crib and watched her drift to sleep, her blue eyes disappearing behind dark lashes and chest moving with deep breaths. As soon as sleep enveloped Alba and her breathing steadied, I stepped into the shower and washed the hospital out of my hair.

I heard a noise from Alba's crib and hurried to feed her. I put her to bed, and went to bed myself, waking up every four hours by alarm to feed Alba, who needed to be bigger by her first doctor's appointment. She was my eternity and I vowed that although she had no father, she would grow up with the love of a mother who cared about her more than anything else.

My mom arrived by plane a week after Alba's birth and gave Alba and me much needed structure and support. We remained in my apartment for the first few weeks after Alba was born, as the nip of winter still hung in the air and Alba remained small. Mom and I spent leisurely days sitting with Alba, playing cards, or cooking. Leo and Marina visited often, growing to love both Alba and my mother. Alba and I rested and grew healthier during those restful days under the watchful eye of my mother, the shadows of exhaustion beneath my eyes giving way and the soft roundness of Alba's belly growing. We organized Alba's Baptism to be on June 4, giving my family time to make travel plans and Alba time to grow. A month after my mother's arrival, she had to go back to work, but said she would be counting the days until her return for Alba's Baptism.

I cautiously began to take Alba outside into the lazy May air for walks. The call of Florence grew too tantalizingly sweet to ignore. Her stroller bumped softly over the cobblestones, the shade of its curtain obscuring her face. In the evenings, when the sun did not twinkle so brightly, Leo and I went on walks with Alba carried in my arms. Sitting on fountain edges with the mist of water sprinkling over us in the cool blues of evening, we discussed literature and history. In preparation for the Baptism, I asked Amelia and Marina to be Alba's godmothers and Mitch to be her godfather.

Alba's cries were seldom, her coos and gurgles often. I loved to sing her to sleep with whatever song was on my mind. I received many visits from my Italian friends, their children showing great interest in Alba. Confused at first, they asked their mothers if they had been that small, but grew more friendly and bold as they watched her intently. They made faces at her, competing for the flick of her pale eyes in their direction.

Alba and I began to go on walks every day, wandering the streets and pushing her baby carriage over the uneven cobblestones. The trees became verdant once more as the long arms of summer embraced the city and the memory of winter disappeared. The city came back to life as if the spring was reaching out to every corner of it, saying with a jaunty laugh, "Wake up, wake up!" The life that surrounded me was in the purple flowers that bloomed from the tables of vendors in the market, it was in the laugh of couples with their arms circling one another, it was the whistled tune of the children who kicked a soccer ball in a side alley. Life in Florence seemed to exist in Technicolor – never black and white – always bright and fast and constantly moving. This bright new life that grew in my heart was ever the more vibrant as I looked at Alba, the life that had come after death – a sort of phoenix, rising from the ashes. Her vivid blue eyes learned to focus on me as her mouth opened in a bubbling smile. Those first months with Alba were both a dream and more real than anything I had ever known at the same time.

Leo visited often with amusing stories about his co-workers and tales of the constellations and mythology, like those that he told his students. I would listen in awe as I cradled Alba in my arms, dreaming of her father up there with the stars. He adored Alba and would play with her for hours on end, not tiring of endless peek-a-boo and letting her hold onto his big hands with her tiny fists. On Fridays, he would bring dinner and we would eat together and then sip espressos while talking about the events of the week.

On the first of June, my twenty-eighth birthday, Leo, Alba, and I planned to go out for a day on the town to celebrate. Leo strode into my apartment with a gleaming smile as I dressed Alba for the sun. I wandered over to Leo and gave him a hug, exclaiming a hello as I danced around the room with Alba, grabbing her hat and dabbing a dot of sunscreen onto her nose. I gently tucked Alba in her baby carriage with light blankets over her little body and we ventured out.

Walking onto the streets of Florence exhilarated me and the warm wind that hinted at summer's enveloping embrace kissed our faces. Alba cooed as the sun reached out to her and touched her alabaster skin. I leaned down and kissed her on the tip of her nose. We ambled over the Ponte Vecchio, greeting beckoning vendors with a happy *"Buongiorno."* Leo led us to the front of the Pitti Palace, where he had taken me when I was in Florence for the first time. Couples sat on the no longer frozen grounds and enjoyed the lovely day, student tourists glanced into the heavens and sneaked peaks at their phones as teachers and guides elaborated upon the history surrounding them. After getting tickets with our Firenze Cards, we strolled into the Boboli Gardens. Leo carried a picnic blanket and set it down as I lifted Alba out of her baby carriage. Then Leo and I sat across from each other, with Alba on my lap, talking about his plans for summer and the book he had been writing.

We sat, amiably talking and laughing. Leo smiled as he reached to pick up Alba and hold her to his chest. She tilted her little head onto his strong shoulder and closed her eyes. His eyes slid shut as he rubbed her back. He kissed Alba on the top of her head, smoothing over her hair. I smiled softly as I watched the two of them, their sweetness and innocence seeping into the air. The green leafiness of the twisting trees hovered above us, lighting the faces of Alba and Leo in a soft haze. Quietly, he cradled her for a moment more and then gently placed her in my arms. I kissed her upturned face.

Leo and I passed Alba between us, talking and laughing until the sun lay low in the sky, still lighting Florence in a soft haze. Alba stirred and smiled slightly as I stood and Leo folded the blanket to walk home. Leo pushed Alba's empty carriage as I walked next to him with Alba in my arms. As we arrived back to my apartment, I placed Alba back in her crib and quietly thanked Leo for the beautiful day. He took a little wrapped gift out of the picnic basket and handed it to me. Thanking him, I gingerly tore the paper to open up the little box. It contained a gorgeous necklace: a pendant of a silver crescent moon inlaid with little crystals dangled from a thin chain. I threw my arms around him in a tight hug and thanked him. He opened the fragile clasp with gentle hands and I lifted my hair as he fastened it around my neck.

I stayed up past midnight, feeding Alba and reading. Early in the morning, I wandered outside, seeing dawn's rosy touch painted across the sky.

Alba rested in my arms, a slight chill coursing around us. Standing, covered in Aaron's robe, I felt deep happiness; my daughter and I were wrapped in the embrace of Florence's tender arms.

Chapter Eight

My family arrived on the four o'clock flight and the moment they spotted me in baggage claim, holding Alba in my arms, they rushed over. Amelia, Mitch and Char, Mom and Dad, and Stacy and John had all come. I introduced them to Alba and they touched her little head and her precious hands. Once their bags had been picked up, Amelia, Alba, and I went towards Marina's little car after I had flagged cabs for my parents, Stacy and John, and Mitch and Char. Amelia would be staying at my apartment, sleeping in my bed while I slept on the couch, and the others would be staying at The Excelsior.

Amelia was in awe at everything – from my apartment to how happy I was. She cuddled Alba while we talked, reminiscing about her own three children as babies, sympathizing with me over the long nights, and giving me advice. Then, yawning with jetlag, she smiled contentedly, hugged me, and went to bed. Alba, who seemed as affected by the excitement of our family visiting as I was, contently remained awake through the night. She simply lay there in my arms; smiling up at me, happy, content not to sleep. Unaffected by anyone else, halcyon moments passed.

Amelia woke up in the middle of the night to find me singing *Beautiful Day* by U2 to Alba. She stood there for a while before I saw her and when I did, I stopped singing. "Please go on," she whispered. When I finished the last notes of the song, she looked at me and murmured, "You are really happy here, aren't you?" I nodded and grinned at her, not saying a word because Alba had finally fallen asleep. I gently rested Alba in her crib and sat cross-legged on the couch next to Amelia. We sat there together silently, lost in our thoughts. After a while, she asked, "How are you really doing without Aaron here?" Resting my cheek on one hand, I responded, "There isn't a day that goes by when he isn't on my mind, when I wonder what it could have been like. All we can do is hope and trust for the future."

The next morning Amelia and I strolled down the street, pushing Alba's carriage, laughing and talking, to meet the rest of our family at The Excelsior. We reached the hotel and our family stood outside, waiting and waving. We hugged each of them and I decided to take them to my favorite café. We sat at an outside table and chatted animatedly, catching up on the last few months. While we sipped espressos and nibbled on flaky pastries, Leo ambled right by us and almost into the café, when my mother promptly cried out, "Leo!" Mom and I hopped up, he hugged us, and we introduced him to our family. He spoke with us for a few minutes, meeting everyone and talking excitedly with them about Alba's Baptism and Florence. Then, he went over to Alba, waved at her as she reached up to grab at his dancing fingers, said goodbye, and left.

Mitch and Char sat talking quietly and laughing. Mitch planted a kiss on the tip of Char's nose and I grinned at their bond, so similar to the closeness that Aaron and I had shared in a time that seemed years before. We finished breakfast and I took them to the market where I had bought the shawl during my first stay in Florence. I introduced them to the old lady who sold shawls. *"Buongiorno!"* she trilled. I returned her happy greeting and we talked in my much-improved Italian while my family shopped. The elderly lady knitter grinned at Alba, chatting to her and reciting the nursery rhymes of her own childhood in a laughing voice, explaining them to me with a smile that lit up her face. My mom and Stacy, both knitters, stroked and examined each shawl's stitches and in the end purchased at least three each as I translated their compliments about how beautiful her work was. She gave us a gummy smile and accepted their money. We left her stall and meandered around the market, the lights strung overhead blinding with the brightness of day.

That evening, we dined at Il Latini, a restaurant in which a person eats more in a single meal than they would normally eat in a day. It was a four-course meal and each was more delicious and filling than the last. We spent the whole evening there, laughing and talking. I drank my first glass of prosecco since my arrival in Italy. Our laughter grew louder and our waiter more friendly. Amelia excitedly told us that she and her children were moving to San Francisco as a prestigious law firm there had hired her. We congratulated her and promised to visit. Alba loved the attention she was given and smiled often, cooing and waving her little fists around in the air.

The stars winked and blinked, flirting as the figures they formed greeted one another and stretched, finally awake in the caravan canopy of darkness. As we promenaded down the street, my mother took a small gift out of her purse wishing me a happy birthday. I handed Alba, who drowsed in my arms, to my dad and opened the gift. It was a tiny locket with a picture of Aaron smiling, his eyes sparking like the sun. I threw my arms around her in a hug and clasped the locket to my breast for a moment before putting it around my neck. A few seconds later, Stacy pulled a gift out of her purse and I unwrapped it, gingerly tearing the paper. Inside lay a gorgeous oriental fan, dotted with rosy cherry blossoms and tender brown branches, with the Chinese character for love written on it from their trip to Asia in March. I grinned and hugged them as we passed along underneath the haze of streetlights. My father handed Alba back to me and she rested against my shoulder, sleeping cuddled against me. I hugged her close and she woke up, looking at me questioningly with her big blue eyes wide open. I laughed and, looking puzzled, Alba fell back asleep.

We arrived home exhausted and after pulling on our pajamas collapsed into our beds. The next morning, Amelia and I woke early to take turns showering and getting ready. I dried my hair and dressed in an emerald green halter neck dress and beige pumps. After that, I carefully dressed Alba in a white gown and combed her hair. Amelia, Alba, and I met the rest of our family at the Excelsior and together we ambled to the little church where the Baptism would be held. I was able to spend time speaking with Stacy and John on the walk and they described their trip to China and Japan, saying how peaceful it had been there and how their hikes through the serene landscapes and visits to monasteries played a large role in their healing process after Aaron's death. We arrived at the church, finding Marina's husband and her three children sitting with Leo in the middle of the church. Marina, my family, and I sat down in the front row and Mass started.

When it was time for Alba to be baptized, we crowded around the baptismal font as Mom snapped pictures, the shudder of her camera blinking in rapid succession. The priest poured the water over Alba's head and she opened her eyes and blinked at him as if to say, "What on earth are you doing?" Then she squirmed and cried out in a high voice. He laughed at her outraged expression and proclaimed, "This one has quite the personality!" He poured water over her twice more and she sputtered a little bit but otherwise appeared no worse for wear. She threw her fists in the air and reached for the priest's microphone. The priest lit the candle, the godparents made their promises, and we all sat back down in our row. "Good job darling," I whispered to Alba. The rest of Mass passed pleasantly and afterwards we stepped out into the warm sunlight, soaking in the boldly bright nature of the day. We strolled to a fancy restaurant for brunch. I ordered Eggs Benedict, wishing that Aaron could be there for such a momentous occasion for Alba.

After brunch, we visited the Duomo and the Uffizi. My art-loving family adored the marvelous paintings and sculptures. In the Botticelli room, we gasped almost simultaneously at the magnificent paintings – many of them including the same mysteriously beautiful woman, both a Madonna and a Venus, her golden waves of hair gently flowing and eyes light with compassion. Down a hallway of sculptures, we tripped over each other, heads turned in various directions from the torqueing body of Laocoön to the proudly serene stare of Minerva. Marina, her husband Vince, and Leo led us around the streets to find the best gelaterias. When we had enjoyed the creamy gelato, I took Alba home for her nap while everyone else visited the Galileo Museum to view such curios as the gnarled and shriveled finger of Galileo himself. While Alba napped, I decided to sleep too and collapsed into my bed where Amelia had slept since she arrived.

Aaron entered my dreams as if he had never left. He came towards me and greeted me. I rushed into his arms and he hugged me close. I could smell his faint, aromatic cologne and ran my hands through his hair. He kissed me the way he had when we were teens: the last kiss before I had to go home – a kiss filled with longing and an unspoken wish for more. He released me after a heavenly eternity and I opened my eyes and peered into his. He smiled, the corners of his lips turning up, and told me, "Look after Alba, love her and know that I love you and miss you every day." He slowly traced a finger down my spine and kissed me once more with all of his strength. We kissed a kiss that the world would stop for, that all life would seize and be still as a statue for. Suddenly, he turned to mist and disappeared, a whisper of the word 'Nicolette' lingering in the air.

When I woke up, I broke down crying. "Aaron, why aren't you here? I need you. I need you more than life itself." My shattering sobs racked through my body, tears staining my cheeks.

Alba woke up and began to cry. I rushed over to her and cradled her in my arms. Alba looked up at me with her tiny brow knit with confusion as my salty tears fell over her face. Finally, I dried my eyes and rested Alba against my breast, her head across my shoulder, rubbing her back with strong hands, "Everything is okay, everything will be okay."

That night, I held Alba, singing to her as I rocked her to sleep in my arms. "Alba," I murmured quietly, "What am I doing? Is this what's right for you?" She breathed out a quiet puff of warm air and let out a tiny noise as she fell asleep.

Alba woke up early and we went out on the balcony to watch the sun rise. I let the slightly chilly breeze pull the embrace of my robe away from my figure, swirling around me like a ball gown. Alba was wrapped up in a blanket and her dark eyelashes blinked over her pale skin. Amelia walked out onto the balcony and stood with me watching the touch of the sun flooding over Florence. "I haven't felt this peaceful in years," Amelia whispered in awe. She closed her eyes and all of the tension and years disappeared from her face. She had the same chestnut hair as me, the color that brought to mind the rippling surface of a towering oak – the oak that has survived a thousand lightning strikes and stands ever stalwart. We stood there together, sisters in love and loss, until the sun was plainly visible in the sky.

With the rest of the family, we left the apartment to meet Marina, her children, and Leo, strolling over the Arno and up the resolute hill that overlooked Florence like a watchful, protective father. We stopped to admire the gorgeous, glinting bronze David. We hiked across fantastic hedges and along soft green grasses. The sun beat down on us, creating red-faced explorers discovering the Italian hills for the first time.

After our little adventure, we traipsed down the cobbled paths to the Boboli Gardens and explored the flourishing, flower-filled fields. Alba fell asleep as we walked and I sat down on a stone bench with her in my arms and her baby carriage next to us. Our family continued a jolly promenade through the gardens, but Leo came and sat with me. He told me that he would have summer break from the University soon and that he planned to visit Slovenia. His eyes lit up as he spoke of the lush beauty of the Slovenian countryside and told me how I must travel there someday. We talked until the shadows began to creep further along the walls. Then, led by Marina, our families marched towards us like a lollygagging, grinning band of soldiers. We left the gardens as the sun set over Florence, hazily leaving a gentle pink silhouette around the buildings.

We dined at a simple, family restaurant, taking many photographs to remember our last dinner in Florence. They all ordered dishes described as superb and I had a hearty *panzanella* salad and *fiori di zucca*. We went back to their hotel, saying goodbye to Marina and Leo. As my mom walked toward the door, she smiled at me quietly saying, "You've done well sweetie." They slipped quietly out the door so as not to wake Alba, who looked like an angel fallen to earth who just happened to be sleeping in my apartment. Amelia and I talked late into the night about everything from frivolous topics such as clothes and makeup to heavy ones of heartbreak and loss. She packed and went to bed and I followed suit.

Early the next morning, I bid my guests farewell in front of the airport as they cooed over Alba one last time and kissed me, thanking me for the time in Florence. I sadly waved goodbye and Alba and I went back to the car. Quietly I murmured to Alba,

"Looks like it's just you and me again Alba." Exhausted after the busy few days, I put fresh sheets on my bed, fed Alba, and rested her in her crib, and fell asleep in a t-shirt.

I woke to the tiny cries of Alba and scooped her up in my arms and fed her. When Alba smiled contentedly at me, I said, "You know what Alba? We're going to go out and have a nice mama and Alba evening tonight." We ambled out into the hazy blue light of dusk. I looked at Alba, whose clear eyes reflected the appearing stars, and kissed her on her little forehead, contemplating where we should go for dinner.

Chapter Nine

The days passed amiably as Alba and I spent our days by the river with Marina and the other children. In mid June, I received a call from Char exclaiming that she and Mitch were going to have a baby in December. Soon I was laughing and congratulating them. Their joy was contagious and I decided to go out for the evening with some friends for a girls' night out. Leaving Alba with Vince, Marina's husband, and their children was difficult, but she slept peacefully and as I kissed her, Vince told me, *"No hanno preoccupazioni!"*

Alba grew stronger, happier to eat, and more mobile. While I cooked or sewed, she would sit contently in her swing, kicking her legs up and down, hands clutching its front. She started to babble when I talked to her and mimic letter sounds that I made. Her smile was bright and beautiful and she grinned toothlessly at almost everyone who passed her. Although she was still small, she was healthy, and I couldn't have been more delighted with her growth.

Leo returned from Slovenia and we met for breakfast at his favorite coffee shop the day after he arrived back in Florence. He caught me in a hug and exclaimed a hello, kissing me on both cheeks. We sat down at a wrought iron table outside and ordered *espresso con panna*. Alba sat in her stroller next to us and Leo played with her while he detailed the adventures of days and sights in Slovenia. He had spent a day by the sea at Piran, three days at Lake Bled, and three days in the capital – Ljubljana. Piran was a lovely seaside town with an old church on the hillside; Leo had hiked up the cobbled streets to the church dedicated to Saint George of dragon-slaying infamy. He attended a Mass there and then relaxed in the dancing breeze outside, watching sunset over the red-shingled roofs and the sparkling sea. He drove from there to Lake Bled where he spent one day simply wandering the trails around the lake and then rowing in a charming wooden boat to a church on an island in the middle of the lake. He described the way that the sun had shone upon the crystal clear lake and the giant fish that resided underneath, lurking and then suddenly breaching the water with a heaving breath. The next day, he visited the castle perched upon a hill, majestic in its stone walls and splendid in its height and views. On the final day, he drove to see the famous caves at Skocjan. A rushing river flowed through the depths of the otherworldly, scantily lit caves filled with stalagmites and stalactites. After visiting the caves, he took a two-hour hike through the forests and other caves with pirouetting waterfalls and snapshots of sun filtering through on the way back to his car. His final stop was Ljubljana. After staying in fairly small, family owned hotels in the other two cities, he stayed in the Hotel Cubo in Ljubljana. It was thoroughly modern and had fantastic city facing views with hints of music wafting through the windows from concerts in a nearby square. In Ljubljana, he spent days meandering the old town, resting at sidewalk cafes, and visiting the castle. The long promenades through the city led up to the castle, culminating in dirt roads and a bridge straight out of Medieval times, propelled him to the castle nearly every day. He sat in squares, eating Slovenia's infamous dark chocolate ice cream, and writing, detailing the sculptures and the dragon bridge and the loves locked onto a bridge with a key thrown into the river for eternity.

I loved listening to his artistic descriptions of Slovenia, a place I now longed to see. I was happy to see him so exuberant; his happiness and lively laugh were infectious. He told me he wanted to take me to the countryside to see the stars because they were most beautiful during the summer. I agreed and we decided to arrange it later.

We spoke more about his trip, our coffee cups long since refilled and emptied again. When the sun met the sky in its midday position, we hugged and parted, promising to go on a walk again later that week.

On the nights that sleep evaded me, I would go to Alba's crib and pick her up, holding her close to me. Her steady breathing warmed my face as I held onto her, my lifesaver in the waves of life. "I love you, I love you," I whispered. Her eyes fluttered open and crinkled in as her mouth released a yawn akin to that of a kitten. I laughed in spite of myself,

"You're beautiful Alba Joy, I wish your daddy was here to see you. He loves you so much and so do I." Her eyes slid shut again and I tucked her back into her crib.

Alba was my life; I spent almost every waking moment with her. During her naps, I found the time to sew and design clothes for her and myself. My favorite store became the textiles shop by our apartment. The bolts of gorgeous, unique fabrics became ready-to-wear clothes in what seemed like the blink of an eye. Growing slowly into more than just a hobby, I started the small business that I had entertained the idea of, based in my apartment, in which I began to do alterations. I fixed the garments that people wanted to love but couldn't find the right fit for: a dress with a drooping waistline, clothes left too large after weight loss, pleats of fabric added to a too small skirt, and similar adjustments. Marina and our other friends helped me to gain clients and soon, I had a bustling little business. Women came to my apartment and showed me the garments and what they wanted done with them. With the profit from this, my New York apartment, my freelance writing, and Aaron's life insurance, Alba and I lived a comfortable life. Together, we became a part of the ever-changing puzzle of Florence.

One weekend, Alba and I took the train up to Milan to look at summer fashions for research for Zola. We sat at cafes on the smooth marble streets and watched the streams of people pass by: crisply dressed businessmen wearing pastel colored cuffed shirts and bright ties, fashionable mothers teetering past in black-heeled sandals and Gucci sunglasses with toddlers perched on their hips, grandmothers with smiling crinkles around their eyes and their grandchildren who pointed into bakeries with multicolored arrays of sweets. As I pushed Alba's stroller down the streets, I looked through the glass panes that sparkled in the early evening light. Gucci, Prada, Miu Miu, Burberry, Versace – each was more splendid than the last. The colors seemed to flow off of the bodies of the mannequins. I wrote snippets of sentences on my phone and compiled and edited them to send to April for the magazine.

We returned to Florence two days later and I felt the familiarity of the city embrace me as our train sped into Santa Maria Novella station. The lazy summer days that followed were sun drenched with a gemstone-toned sky. Alba learned to propel herself upwards with resolute arms and eventually to turn over. The days passed as the buzz of the air conditioning hummed in tune to the steady beat of my sewing machine. The tune looped and looped each day, the peak of the song in the evening when we ventured onto the streets, the hum turning into a crescendo of noise and voices and laughter. Those were the best parts of the summer, wandering down streets with Alba, dinners with Leo, and espresso with Marina. The days blur, but I can clearly remember the laughter and joy.

Chapter Ten

The bliss of summer danced through the city and I felt myself caught up in the fancy-free twirl. Leo, Alba, and I went out to dinner or lunch at least twice a week. Gleefully escaping into the coolness of a restaurant or sitting outside under the light mist of fans, we laughed and talked. My heart lightened as we joked and talked about life. I found myself thinking about him more and more.

In the moments away from my work, I decided to take up painting again. Early in August, I found an art shop in a small alley near the Uffizi and bought canvases and a few new tubes of vibrant paint. Engaged in my artwork while Alba napped or sat bouncing contently in her baby swing, I spent tranquil hours on my balcony trying to perfect a scene of the Arno and Ponte Vecchio. In between sewing jobs, I started working on a more modern-esque painting, one of a woman, her face obscured in many colors of paint with streaks like tears down her face. Her eyes peeked out, strong and hopeful amidst the chaos around. Leo would sit with me as I painted and write his book on his laptop, the two of us sitting in amiable silence. His presence while I painted was peaceful, unquestioning, and relaxed.

The steady filter of my clients bringing clothes for alterations became as typical as the swift breeze through the windows. I arranged a corner of the living room into a hall of mirrors with a paneled off dressing area behind them. These women grew to be more than customers, becoming friends with every fitting, every stitch, and every story. Histories behind the clothes were astounding: from an inherited ball gown a grandmother had worn to a prince's ball in the 1930s, hewn from silk and carefully draped, but with threads in the hem tearing, to a pair of ivory gloves passed to each bride in a woman's family since the 1950s, now with a gaping hole in the palm and pale stains on the wrists. The business grew from my love of designing, but thrived in the love of the people that came. Each person and story became part of the fabric of my new life.

With the Florentine heat and constant influx of work, I barely had time to tend to my very long hair. Ever since my teens, my hair had reached halfway down my back – or more depending on the year. Its length had given me versatility as a model, but as a mother, it was insensible. In September, at the age of twenty-eight, I finally decided to cut my hair short. I left Alba with Marina, thanking her but not saying my plans. I selected a salon and asked if anyone was available to cut my hair. Having had a cancellation, the owner offered me a slot right away, "How much do you want off?" I replied that I wanted a complete change to a short style that would frame my face. I asked that the hair cut off be given to an Italian version of Locks of Love that was advertised in the front window. He led me over to the hair-washing station. The hairdresser's assistant washed my hair, the pounding of the water drizzling through my thick locks. Next, the hairdresser led me over to a swivel chair; I calmly watched as feet of hair cascaded to the floor. My face slowly transformed with each layer that fell away.

I barely recognized myself and I loved it. The shorter hair gave me a more sophisticated air. My new hairstyle went just past my chin in a light bob, a fashion that flattered my elfin face perfectly. Little layers peeked out and my naturally highlighted hair glowed. The hairdresser came over to me and kissed me on both cheeks like an old friend and said, "Come back again!"

As I walked back to my apartment, my head felt lighter than it had in years. I dressed in a flaring, *limoncello* colored dress with thin straps and an empire waist with black stiletto heels, wanting to look as bright and fancy-free as I felt. I went to Marina's apartment to find Leo sitting on the floor, playing with Alba. He looked up when I walked in and gasped. "Your hair?" he stuttered. I spun around, the skirt of my dress flaring and my light hair flowing around me to settle in the perfect spot. "What do you think?" I asked with a smile. He simply strode over, put his arms around my waist, and kissed me.

I felt my heart speed up and start tap-dancing in my chest. I melted into his soft embrace. His hands gently touched my hair. I heard a gasp from the edge of the kitchen and we parted to find Marina standing and grinning at the edge of the room. "Finally!" she exclaimed with a laugh, "And your hair looks fantastic!" Then, thinking for a moment, she offered generously, "Why don't you two go somewhere nice for dinner and I'll watch Alba." Leo and I looked at each other and agreed that we would love to.

Leo and I walked, talking about our days and laughing amiably. We reached a small building near the Duomo with gorgeous frescoes across the front. There was a staircase down to a door, surrounded by bougainvillea in full bloom and traced by a wrought iron railing with a 'fleur de lis' motif. Leo opened the door for me and led me in.

The restaurant was built around Roman-era ruins with shining marble columns spread throughout it. We were seated aside a painting of the muses displaying their assorted talents from the heights of Olympus and above a glass floor that looked onto more ruins beneath us. In Florence layers and layers of history overlap, mingling to create something beautiful.

Leo and I sat quietly as I studied my menu intently, my eyes glancing up to meet his reassuring gaze every now and then. He grinned at me and I reached across the table and took his hand; he squeezed mine, his dark eyes sparkling with a new light.

When we left the restaurant, he clasped my hand and we traversed through the night-shimmering streets to the waterfront and sat on the bridge. The stars sparkled as brightly as if they had been made days, not eons, ago. My favorite guitarist, Claudio, had set up his music, stood on the pavement, and started to play and sing 'Viva La Vida' by Coldplay. Leo stood and helped me up, pulled me into his arms, and we swayed to the music. Other couples joined in until no one could walk across the bridge without having to cross the paths of the dancers. Many gave up, joined in, and began to dance. Giggling teenaged girls stood with their arms around each other, swaying. A bride and groom, rushing through the city with their entourage, stopped and began to dance, the bride's white dress fluttering around her with the grace of dove's wings. *This* was the magic of Italy – the magic in the love, the carefreeness, the idea of a romance that could come at any minute like the breezes that blow across Tuscany: lovely, tender, fleeting, and slightly reminiscent.

The final strains of the song flowed from Claudio's guitar and older couples sat down tenderly. The bride and groom held hands and continued their journey through Florence. The teenaged girls headed to a gelato shop, staring smugly at soulful-eyed teenaged Italian boys as they went. Leo went to drop a twenty-euro note in the velvety guitar case and whispered something to Claudio. Claudio began to play the familiar first verse of 'Hey Soul Sister' by Train, my favorite song, and I looked at Leo and grinned. He looked back at me. "Do you know how to swing dance?" I asked him, he smiled and said, "Know how? I am *un maestro!*"

We started the fast dance, our feet frenzied in the steps: right, left, back, spin. An elderly couple smiled on at us as we kept up the quick pace of the dance. When the song finished and we stopped dancing, people applauded, their sparkling eyes laughing with the simple pleasure of night, light, and love. Claudio laughed and smiled, gesturing at us. I curtsied with a laugh and Leo bowed, the full moon smiling at our antics as he embraced the Arno, pulling her slender undulating form in their own age-old dance, the golden buildings of Florence boldly watching with parental supervision of this nightly rendezvous.

I fell asleep that night with a smile on my face, my feet still tracing the steps of the dance, my heart still reflected in the eyes of the moon, laid bare in open joy under the haze of street lights.

The next day, I woke up with the rising of the sun to feed Alba. Her inquisitive eyes fixed on me as she cuddled against my breast. I looked into Aaron's eyes, so plainly imprinted on the face of our child. In those eyes, I could see her future, a future of love, dedicated in the name of her father. I could see her standing tall and strong, the fiery confidence of Aaron running through her blood.

Marina, her children, and Leo visited us that afternoon. We sat in the kitchen sipping espressos and laughing and talking as the children giggled and played on the floor.

Warmth.

That is the description that comes to mind when I think of that day, the sweet crackle of warmth that emanated from within. Leo playfully leaned over at one point and asked me if I wanted to go out for dinner that night. A little while later, Leo excused himself, saying to me that he would pick me up around seven o' clock. Marina smiled mischievously at me and told me that she would be happy to do babysitting duty any and every night if Leo and I were together.

After she had left, I fed Alba, and while she napped, took a shower. I then walked to Alba's crib, leaning over and tracing her cheek. I whispered in her ear how much I loved her, the sound of her breathing like gentle music to my ears. She made a small noise in her sleep and kicked her feet for a second. In that moment I made a wish for her, one that I longed to have learned much earlier in my life. I pleaded in whisper to her, "Learn happiness, love yourself, and always know that you are loved, most of all by me. Live like your father did, vividly alive and always having fun whatever he did, and know that you can be your perfect self. This life is yours to create."

I dressed and applied my makeup in a relaxed manner, soaking in the sun that flooded through my windows. I let my hair dry in the light breeze that swished in through my open balcony doors. I danced around the house and picked Alba up and spun her around in the air just like Aaron would have if he were there. Her cries turned into squeals.

I pulled her down into a big embrace as I walked with her into the kitchen and put her in her baby carriage to take her to Marina, kissing her head lightly and smiling as she wrapped her hands around the hair that fell in front of my face.

Leo stood waiting on Marina's balcony, a streetlight flickering on as the light of day slowly disappeared. The setting of the sun reflected in his dark eyes, lighting them with golden fragments. He took my hand in his strong one and together we made our way down the street.

That night, we dined at a tiny restaurant that couldn't have had more than four or five tables. We ate a perfect pizza and a molten chocolate cake, oozing with the black gold of chocolate. We stayed talking and discussing the news and the world with our hands entwined.

A waiter came over and coughed delicately. We were broken out of our exchange as Leo handed the man a credit card. We left as the first drops of rain plinked and plunked across the sidewalk. We walked through the rain, laughing as we ducked through it with no umbrella, wrapped up in the freshness of rain after the muggy summer heat. We clung to one another's hands, obliviously carefree in the liberation of rain. Finally, when our skin was dewy and our hair damp and disheveled, we found ourselves at the door to my apartment building. We ended the evening with a hug underneath the awning in front of the apartment building and I ran upstairs to pick up Alba.

Marina hugged me goodnight as she gave me Alba in her baby carriage and then I walked to my apartment, exhausted from the events of the last two days. Alba's soft eyes flew open and she raised her hands in to the air towards me. I leaned down, soft tufts of my hair dripping, and kissed her forehead. Her eyes fluttered closed again and I gently moved her from her baby carriage to her crib. I pulled off my wet clothes, and dried my hair until it softly floated around my face in a halo of warmth. I dragged a t-shirt over my head and collapsed exhaustedly into my bed.

Chapter Eleven

Alba's tears and hungry cries woke me at some ungodly hour when all I craved were the nutrients of sleep. For the hundredth time, I wished that I had a husband to share these midnight rendezvous with Alba. I awoke again at eight to feed her and once again fell back asleep as she did.

I woke up what seemed like minutes later to Marina's puppy-like brown eyes hovering above me. "Nicolette? Are you okay?" The room spun around me like a merry-go-round and my legs buckled out from under me, as I tried to stand. The world faded to black and blessed sleep consumed me. I lay there, hot then cold, flashing between sleep and alertness. Leo gripped my hand, his eyes worn and concerned, and then disappeared. I remembered a doctor being quietly led into the room and being given medicine in a feverish haze of visions and words.

The next night, Marina told me that I had had a raging fever and the doctor had prescribed medicines and rest. Marina told me that she had been watching Alba and taking care of her. I thanked her profusely for that, tremendously grateful in knowing that Marina would always be there for my daughter and me.

Leo rushed into my apartment when he heard that I was awake and knelt by the bed. His fingers stroked my hand with the lightest of touches and his head drooped forward for a second until it hovered above the covers. We sat there, our hands entwined tightly and I drifted off to sleep. I woke up to see him, eyes drooping shut but spine rigid, watching me from a plush chair in the corner of my room. A faint smile grew on my face and he strode over to me. He pressed his lips to my hand, "Are you okay?" I nodded and my head sunk back into the pillows.

I was glad to have Alba back with me the next day and feeling much better, I got out of bed and went to hold Alba and stand on our deck. I felt better the minute my baby was in my arms and I clutched her to me, never wanting to be away from her again. Leo came by and happy to see me up and about, kissed me on the forehead. Finding myself in desperate need of a bit of sun and fresh air, I asked Leo if he would come on a walk with us. He kindly agreed and I changed into a flowing blouse and jeans and pinned my hair back. I dressed Alba into a pink and white onesie and brushed her dark hair.

I strapped Alba into her stroller and Leo pushed the stroller. He maneuvered with one hand and crooked his other arm, letting me lace my arm through his as we wandered through the streets. With the burst of sun pushing away the lightheadedness of my illness, I felt immediately better. The day was perfection itself; the sun's gift of warmth and energy seemed to flow around us. We pleasantly strolled through the streets, not needing to say anything, for whatever was lacking in the conversation was plentiful in simple happiness to be together. At some point as we were walking, he took his hand out from where it had been linked with mine and slid it around my waist.

Feeling stronger and better the next day, Leo and I went for a walk after a leisurely late lunch at the market. We started walking again each evening, for longer and longer periods of time until I was back to my old vigor. Alba was always happy to be outside, waving to everyone we passed on the cobblestone streets and babbling happily to strangers who peeked into her stroller. She seemed just as happy indoors, close to me while I began to work on my sewing again. I followed up with the women who were still waiting for their alterations, finished and delivered them, and I restarted work on a painting. Our lives went on and in the shadow of the ancient buildings of Florence, it seemed that neither the sun nor life had ever shone more brightly.

Chapter Twelve

On September third, we had a little party for Alba's five-month birthday and for a treat I fed her fruit purée. For the adults and older children present – Leo, Marina, Vince, Gian, Marco, Bella, and me – I made cucumber sandwiches and petit fours. I doubt Alba had any idea what was going on, but she giggled and played, pleased with even more attention than usual.

Alba uttered her first word near the end of September, looking quizzically at me as she solemnly said, "Mama." My mouth fell open as I kissed her on the forehead, filled with joy, and hugged her as tightly as I could. I prompted her to say it again. I could never get enough of her tiny voice, as clear as a bell, calling out to me. In celebration, I decided to take her out and around the Boboli Gardens adjoining the Pitti Palace, which she adored. I pushed her stroller as she waved her chubby hands at anyone who would look at her. The other walkers all waved back at her and cooed to me how adorable she was.

Alba grew more with each passing day. She cried a little more often and I realized that I could see the tips of tiny teeth coming out of her gums. Alba loved it when I rubbed her gums and she would sigh contentedly and smile brightly. Whenever she wanted me, she learned to say 'Mama.' She hardly ever frowned and always grinned or made happy noises. Marina's children proved to be great friends to her and were always happy for another game of peekaboo.

As Alba grew, so did my relationship with Leo. He visited most days after work and corrected coursework on my balcony while I painted or sewed. Alba would nap or sit in her baby swing by the door, where both of us could keep a close watch on her. Even though I probed Leo about the novel he was writing, he still wouldn't tell me anything about the plotline. He simply told me that he needed to extend the date for its publication and that it was not going as quickly as he had hoped. This made me wonder even more about its subject, but I was left in suspense.

September's gaiety morphed into the soft clarity of October and the winds of Tuscany flowed ever more coolly. One day, we spent the evening in the countryside. Marina lent Leo her car late one afternoon and offered to keep Alba for the evening. We drove over the bumpy roads until we arrived at a sun-dappled hill where the wind's song made the grass dance with pleasure. Below the grassy slope was a clear lake where the sun shone through the waters giving clarity to its very depths. Near the top of the hill, Leo laid out a picnic blanket and set up a cooler with a bottle of prosecco in it. He took out a container of salad, *penne alla vodka*, and two slices of lemon cake.

Leo helped me onto the blanket as my vintage 1950s black skirt swirled around my calves. I slid off my shoes and sat down next to Leo. The lake glimmered with the pink clouds of sunset, the tangerine sky melting into the waves. The sun fell, head wilting beneath the mountains and leaving the golden waves of her hair to softly fall behind her until the sky was masked in the intricate veil of night, diamonds shining on its deep blue velvet. We ate the meal contentedly and afterwards, we lay back on the blanket and he named the constellations for me. He recounted countless stories of the mythology behind each. Every story was poetic and I simply let the stars imprint themselves in my memory as I listened to his melodic voice tell the tales of times passed.

Suddenly, Leo looked at his watch and glanced back at me. He tilted my chin up to the skies and a shooting star swam across the sky – bright and vivid. "Look Nicolette, see the stars; they will be your guide through the nights and light your way to sunrise. They are present even when you don't see them. Make a wish." I closed my eyes and thought of my dearest wishes. Then I opened my eyes, tilting my head to look at Leo, the stars reflected in his deep eyes. I leaned in towards him, and whispered in his ear, "Here is my wish," and kissed him. We lay there on the blanket together. I stayed wrapped up in his arms and his voice tickled my ear, "I love you." It seemed so natural that before I could even think, I responded, "I love you too." He pulled me even closer towards him and we lay there as the breeze kicked up and blew around us.

In his arms, I knew that I was safe from whatever storms were to come.

As we drove back into Florence that night, I switched between radio stations while he drove. He held the steering wheel with one hand and took my hand with the other. Words cannot explain how at peace I felt. We arrived at my apartment and he helped me out of the car and walked with me to Marina's apartment. He told me he didn't want to disturb Marina so he hugged me and made his way back downstairs while I picked up Alba.

Alba grew quickly and so did her vocabulary. At six-and-a-half months, it included Mama, Ally, Leo, *ciao*, Mari, bye, and yay. We had daily conversations, with me speaking to her in English and her listening keenly and responding with one-word exclamations or noises.

Alba's hair grew longer and her limbs lengthened and grew happily plump. Aaron was still an unseen presence in my life, but he was no longer always my first thought or the only one in my mind. Around my neck hung both the necklace that Leo had given me for my twenty-eighth birthday and the necklace that held Aaron's ring.

Chapter Thirteen

November came with a biting cold as the Florentines took to wearing their stylishly wrapped and fitted coats. Scarves are an essential in the Florentine winter and are worn wrapped over their heads and around their necks in various styles. The kidskin and leather fur-lined gloves, sold at markets and fashion stores alike, sat patiently on their stools and shelves, waiting to be plucked up by the reddened fingers of the cold. I wrote my column for *The Ray* on the warm colors and smooth, soft fabrics of the Florentine winter.

The first snow fell in mid-November and I took Alba outside wrapped in blankets and a jacket. Never having seen snow, she adored the softness of the little puffs of snow falling upon her face. We sat on the balcony, Alba in my warm arms, surrounded by a soft pillow of snow. Alba grabbed a handful of just fallen snow, and before I could stop her, stuck it in her mouth. She opened her eyes wide and drew in a breath. I laughed as I took her inside, making sure that she was okay.

All of the snow on the streets gave me plenty of time inside and the more snow I saw, the more homesick I felt missing my parents, siblings, and friends. I planned an almost month long trip back to America that would coincide perfectly with the birth of Char and Mitch's baby and the holidays.

Alba and I would leave on December 5 from Florence to Paris and then take the long flight from Paris to San Francisco. I would stay there, with Amelia, who had just moved there, until mid-December. Then I would visit Mitch and Char, my parents, and Stacy and John until January 2nd in New York. Excitedly, I called my family, telling them of my visit and informing them of the dates I would be there.

Marina watched Alba while Leo and I went walking in the snow. His brown leather-clad hand clutched my black-covered one as we made our way through the snowy streets. I slid on a patch of ice and he put a hand around my waist to steady me as we continued our trudge through the snow. I tilted my head against his shoulder, closing my eyes as I soaked in his peace. After the cold seemed to have burned through our very skin, we trudged into the café where we had first met. We gripped our hot chocolates and let their warmth seep into our icy hands. When the heat from the mugs had receded, we drank the warm, thick liquid.

Many days in November, Alba, Leo, and I went walking through Florence in the snow. All that peeked out of the bundle of blankets that was Alba were her mouth, nose, and eyes. She freed her pink clad hands and fingers and raised them into the air, grabbing at elusive flickers of snow. The thick smell of meat hovered in the air, hesitantly leaning across the streets from the thin gaps of butcher's shop doors. Waffle cones, baked to golden perfection, emitted their softly sweet smell, dancing with the hazy waves of chocolate gelato. Thin wisps of espresso split the air, pushing for attention, throwing aside daintiness and niceties. Vendors sat enveloped in plaid blankets, curled over on stools. Horses, strapped to carriages, tapped impatient feet, breath suspended in slender silhouettes and bodies hidden under thick covers. A glassy silence hung in the air, the music of Florence slowly humming, pausing, rewinding – making its way back to the beginning of the track.

Wrapped in soft blankets, Leo and I passed our evenings together in front of the popping, sashaying fire, watching Alba play or holding her and speaking and playing with her. Leo spent his days lecturing at the university – teaching two classes and meeting with his graduate students. His evenings passed at my side, grading and writing. My days spun with the spool of my sewing machine, the threads of conversations with Marina and clients, and the strokes of paint on canvas. I wrote snippets about fashion and pooled together pictures of the styles into a scrapbook to emulate. I busily kept an album for Alba on her milestones and with pictures of our little family, smiling with the thought of her as a young woman, carefully flipping through the pages to look into the past.

Thanksgiving Day, a holiday not celebrated in Italy, came on November 25th. I cooked a turkey, mashed potatoes, cranberry sauce, pumpkin pie, and various salads and invited all of my Italian friends over. We sat at the large oak table, bowing our heads as one of Leo's close friends, a priest, blessed the food. Alba sat in a place of honor on my lap at the head of the table as I fed her pumpkin purée with a cracker that she gnawed at with her few teeth in celebration. Everyone loved the meal and as we poured Prosecco, I stood. In my finally perfected Italian, I cleared my throat and said, "On this day, we say thanks for all of our blessings. So I will start." I paused for a moment as everyone thought of their blessings and I spoke up again, saying, "I am grateful for you - my amazing friends, my family in America, my life here in Florence, my perfect baby, Alba, for the brilliant friend and sister that Marina is, and for Leo."

Marina spoke next, "I am grateful for my dear friends, especially the beautiful people here, my great husband, and my *bambini*, including the one that I will be having next August." We all gasped in surprise and congratulated her, smiling at her news and rushing to hug her. Leo stood after his sister sat and the congratulations ceased and said, "I am grateful for my family, for my job, and for my writing; I am most especially grateful for the presence of Nicolette and Alba in my life." I smiled widely and leaned over from my seat to his and hugged him.

The thanking and counting of blessings that followed came in many tones, varying from silly to sincere. After everyone had eaten their fill, I turned on speakers playing holiday music. We all danced around and I held Alba as we swayed to the music. 'I'll Be Home for Christmas' started to play with the warm, crackling sound reminiscent of gramophones and jukeboxes past. Marina took Alba from me and Leo pulled me into his arms and we danced slowly. Out of the corner of my eye, I saw Marina place Alba in her crib and after that, her husband took her in his arms. I smiled, knowing how lucky I was to have two families: my American family and my adopted Italian family. We danced for about an hour and as children became sleepy-eyed, their yawning parents slowly filtered out of the doors. I held Alba to find her eyes drifting closed and cuddled with her as we said our goodbyes. Everyone left, wishing us a Happy Thanksgiving.

My final guests left around midnight, leaving Leo, Alba, and myself. He kissed the top of my head and I slipped out of his arms for a moment. I laid Alba in the crib, kissed her on the forehead, and I walked over to Leo, who was lying down on the thick carpet in front of the flickering fire. His head rested in his crossed arms and strands of dark hair fell forward onto his face. He slowly turned on his side, a drowsy smile on his face. I lay down next to him and put my arms around his neck, resting my head on his shoulder as he played with my hair, gently twirling and twisting it in and out of his tapering fingers. We rested like that for a lengthy, peaceful time and slowly my eyes slid shut.

I woke up to find Leo gently picking me up and laying me down on the couch as the first peaks of dawn shone through the windows. I wrapped my arms around his neck and tilted my head onto his chest. He tenderly laid a blanket over me and kissed my forehead, "Good morning Nicolette and goodbye, I will see you later today." He bent down once more and kissed my lips. He quietly slipped out the door and I turned over, wandering to sleep once more.

Alba woke up and exclaimed my name, shaking the plushness of sleep off of me and propelling me towards her. Wrapping the blanket around my shoulders, I grinned at her and picked her up to give her breakfast. After her delicious feast of yam purée, I put her on the floor in the living room on a blanket with some learning toys and helped her to play with and organize them. I sang quietly as Alba giggled, flipping through the cardboard pages of a book. The door boomed with a knock.

I jumped up and called Marina in, hugging her and congratulating her again. We decided to go out to celebrate her pregnancy. Alba and Marina's four-year-old daughter, Bella, came with us, bundled in coats and grinning at the cleared skies. Marina and I ordered cappuccinos, Bella ordered pear juice, and Alba happily sipped milk from her bottle. When we had caught the last drops of cappuccino and eaten the tinted foam with dainty spoons, we pulled on our velvety coats, caps, and scarves and journeyed back into the chilly weather.

Marina took Bella's mitten-covered hand and I pushed Alba's baby carriage as we meandered through the streets together. Marina and I chatted as Bella spoke in her almost perfect sentences to Alba. We reached our apartments and I excused myself to pack for our trip. I took out one of the medium-sized suitcases that I had travelled with when I first moved to Italy.

December came with a snowstorm that dimmed the city with a fog of white, obscuring the sun and the moon and the stars. Leo and I stood on my balcony bundled in thick quilts and watched the Arno become ice and little children throwing snow at one another. Leo pulled me closer under the blanket and I laughed as he pressed a cold hand to my face. He swung his arm around my shoulders and we watched the icicles drip puddles and crevices into the snow. He grinned, "I made dinner tonight. Come over." I bent my head to his shoulder and told him that Alba and I would love to.

We put on our coats and I wrapped Alba in her little coat and blankets. The three of us ventured out into the streets, the ice hidden beneath a powdery layer of snow crunching under the treaded soles of our boots. We walked through the city to his apartment, took off our winter outer layers, and sat down across from each at his small square table. Alba sat in a high chair and Leo put some Cheerios on the dish part of the chair and placed a bowl of puréed pears in front of her. He proceeded to feed her the pear, burp her, and put her back in the chair to play with and nibble on Cheerios.

As Alba giggled and grabbed at the evasive Cheerios, Leo took out our meal. He set up a tossed salad of vinaigrette, peppery arugula, candied walnuts, champagne dressed pears, and goat cheese. We savored each bite, intermittently sipping from glasses of fruity white wine. For the main meal, he brought out a thick potato soup. We spoke of our holiday plans as we dined. He said that he was going up to Milan to see his mother and father for Christmas. After that, he was coming by train back to Florence. His parents planned to follow him back to Florence to spend a month visiting their children and grandchildren. He said that he wanted them to meet me when I came back from America. Leo disappeared into the kitchen.

Leo entered the room with a container of tiramisu, the same one we had learned to make together at the Italian cooking class the first time we met. We dished the espresso-laced treat onto our plates and gingerly ate the crumbling, soaked ladyfingers and cream. When we had finished our portions and our wine glasses sat glistening, empty, under the dim lights, I dressed Alba in all of her coats, buttoned up my blue trench coat, and pulled my knit cap over my tousled hair. We traipsed home together, Leo insisting on accompanying us directly to our door. I kissed him goodnight, thanking him for the wonderful evening.

The next morning I went to have my hair cut again as it had grown out rather quickly to my shoulders. The hairdresser cut it in practically the same manner as the first time but with more layers. Alba sat happily giggling as the other hairdressers and their clients played peekaboo with her. We went home and I put Alba in the sink for her bath. She happily splashed and played with the bubbles as I washed her with baby soap. Afterward, I cut her small but sharp nails and trimmed her hair. With my errands for the day complete, I went to work on alterations and left Alba sleeping in her crib.

Later that day, I left Alba with Marina and went to meet Leo at the University. I walked through the bright halls, watching the students hurry past me in the endless rush to arrive on time for class. I strolled leisurely towards Leo's office and peeked in through the window in the door to see him sitting with two or three students. The door opened and Leo's head popped out, "Hey Nicolette! We're almost done, come in!" I stepped into the office and the students greeted me happily. I smiled as Leo introduced me, "Guys, this is Nicolette. Nicolette this is Stefano, that's Lucia, and this is Francisco." Each waved as their name was said and Stefano laughed, "We've heard all about you Nicolette. What a pleasure!" I laughed in return. Leo quickly wrapped up with the students, "Well, I think that's everything, if you have any more questions, just email me; I think it's about time that I go to lunch with Nicolette." He waved at them and they all told him to have fun and grinned at me as they left. He shut the door to his office and I giggled, "Leo, you're practically one of them. I bet they thought that you were a student on your first day!" He laughed and nodded.

We strolled through the hallways and I took his hand, saying, "How much time do we have until your next class?" "I'd say about an hour and a half; I think that's quite enough time to eat lunch." We tripped along, as giddily as students playing hooky, down the street, in search of a café.

Chapter Fourteen

The night of the anniversary of Aaron's death, I sat awake, moving from my bed to in front of the fire and back again, restless all night, thinking about the changes that had occurred over the last year. Midnight came and passed; Aaron had died around this time exactly a year ago. I pressed my nose against the window, one cheek hardened against the cold pane, the other burning with the gentle undulations of heat flowing from the fireplace. Ghosts of snowflakes eerily flitted past the window. My tears were cool relief as they slipped down my face; yet an eerie sense of peace enveloped me. Aaron could never be at my side, but he would always be with me, in spirit and in Alba. He was omnipresent; he would guide Alba through her life, but I still found my heart aching with missing him. Alba's cries pierced the night. I rushed to her and held her to my chest, sharing in all of the comfort and sweetness of her small, warm body. My tears dripped down onto her head and she looked at me, puzzled, as if to say, "I'm supposed to be crying, not you!" I stood there with her and the nothingness of night that seeped into my apartment through the windows and I whispered into the darkness, "Here we are Aaron, one year later. I'm in Florence and have our baby. I still miss you just as much as I did one year ago. I will always love you no matter where I am. I wish you were here."

Alba had fallen asleep again and I carried her into her bedroom and tucked blankets around her until I was sure she would feel none of the coldness of the aching world. I whispered stories of her father, stories that I would tell her over and over again when she could remember them, stories that she would know her father through. I wandered back to the window, staring out into the bleak darkness until I found the first lights of dawn. They shone down on me, illuminating my adopted home and carrying it to life.

I took Alba to Mass when the sun started its hike into the blue trail of sky. I sat contemplatively through Mass with Alba cuddled in my arms. At some point during the sermon she drank the bottle of milk I had brought. I went through the motions of the Mass, mentally having to remind myself, "Bow. Kneel. Sing. Pray." I imagined Aaron sitting next to me, marveling at the frescoes on the ceiling and asking me jokingly if I thought that he could imitate them. At the 'kiss of peace' he would have hugged me and kissed me on the lips and he would have taken Alba out of my arms and lifted her in the air, making her giggle. I shook my head to clear it of the images so realistically created and the old man seated next to me gave me a kind smile. He nudged over towards me and patted Alba on the head, remarking how cute she was and blessed her forehead saying, "Peace is already with this little one."

I walked out of Mass and re-bundled Alba in the many blankets I had unwound her from. We took the elevator up to Leo's apartment and I knocked on the door. Leo came to the door, opening it with a drowsy smile. Alba's soft, sleeping breath sounded as I pushed her stroller next to the couch. Leo and I sat on the plush couch, "Are you okay Nicolette?" My eyes closed and a tear slid out, "Today is the one year anniversary of Aaron's death." "Oh, Nicolette," he murmured and put his arms around me. I rested against his firm chest and he tenderly ran his hands through my hair and down my back until they stopped and encircled my waist. I leaned against him and my head dropped back against his shoulder. My tears turned to sobs and Leo held me, bracing me against the storm that was flowing out of and around me. I stuttered between sobs, "I can't believe he's gone Leo. He was too young. Why couldn't Alba have known him?" He turned my face to his and touched my cheek, his brown eyes flooded with sadness, "I'm so sorry Nicolette." I put my head against his shoulder, "No one deserves to die at twenty-seven." My breath came in starts, tearing out of my chest. I sniffled into his shirt, "I'm sorry." I felt his voice vibrate in his chest, murmuring words that I couldn't make out. Slowly, my tears and sadness faded to numbness.

Alba awoke and after an espresso together to nurse my raw emotion, Leo helped me to strap Alba into her stroller and walked us home. When we reached my apartment, Leo walked us to the door. He picked up Alba and said, "Goodbye Alba! Leo will miss you!" He kissed her forehead and spun her around one final time. Then Leo took me in his arms. We stood there hugging, not saying a word, for a minute or two. He leaned down and pressed his lips to mine. When we separated, I whispered, "We'll be back sooner than you know. I love you Leo." He squeezed my hand and murmured, "I love you too Nicolette."

That evening, Marina came over to my apartment with some cookies wrapped up for my trip. She had helped me to finish final alterations. I had told my customers that I was going out of country and would be back to work in January. Marina's eyes were bright and she exclaimed, "Enjoy your time with your family. It is always good to go home." I replied, "This too is my home now, Marina." She grinned and hugged me close.

My alarm rang at seven a.m. and Alba and I slid into a cab with our suitcase and backpack. Alba happily sat on my lap for the whole flight to Charles de Gaulle Airport in Paris, but the flight to San Francisco was a nightmare. She cried intermittently. The old woman next to me looked at me disapprovingly and sighed. I closed my eyes and took a deep breath, holding Alba close to me once more in an effort to calm her.

The hours on the plane dragged by; I had never been more relieved than when the plane jolted onto the ground. My exhaustion turned to excitement as I found a taxi to take Alba and me to Amelia's apartment. Amelia ran out the door and wrapped me in a hug, kissing Alba on the forehead. "Auntie Nicolette and Alba are here!" she called to her children. They ran down the stairs, the fastest being the youngest, my six-year-old goddaughter, Sunny. Her little arms wrapped around my legs and Amelia took Alba so I could hug all of them. Amelia's other two children, Helena and Avril, ran over and enveloped me saying, "We've missed you Auntie!"

The children all cooed over Alba as she grinned and babbled at them. While Alba was extremely busy meeting her new and very interesting cousins, Amelia and I sat down in two chairs facing them. We discussed her move to San Francisco, her job, and her new friends, and my relationship with Leo, my business, and Alba's growth. After a lovely dinner and putting the girls to bed, we pulled sheets across the sofa bed and threw a quilt over it. I hugged Amelia again and fell asleep in the blink of an eye.

The next morning, I woke up to Sunny poking my arm and exclaiming, "I'm going to school! I wanted to say bye!" I picked her up and spun her around. She squealed with delight as I put her down and kissed her on the tip of her nose, "Goodbye Sunny, I love you!" I went over to Helena and Avril and gave each of them a kiss on the cheek and helped them tug on their puffy jackets. Amelia was sitting in a plush chair in her living room, holding Alba's hands and bouncing her up and down on her knees. Alba giggled as the exciting ride finished and Amelia handed her to me. Amelia gave me a kiss on the cheek and told me,

"I'm going to work now. The kids return at three-thirty by bus and I should be home by five at the latest. I wish I could stay home and spend time with you, but I have to present the final arguments for this case." She slung a scarf around the neck of her well-cut black jacket. As she slid on her heels, she told me, "We are hoping that the case will rest today, wish me luck!" I did just that as she ran out the door and into her car.

Alba and I bundled up in our coats and stepped outside. Walking up and down the steep streets of San Francisco in the burning cold and pushing Alba's stroller was as good an exercise as any. Finally, with calves aching, we stopped at a Ghirardelli and I ordered a Caramel Hot Chocolate. Alba happily sipped warm formula from a Sippy-cup that an employee had helpfully heated. We strolled to the piers and ambled around there, listening to the sound of the ocean and smelling the wafting fragrances from various crepe stands and curry restaurants, sultry and sweet, seductively tangoing through the air, enticingly pulling walkers into their dance. The gray waves tossed stormily, but the sky shone startlingly clearly. With the breeze kicking up and the clouds blowing across the bay, we hiked back to Amelia's house.

That night before bed, I carried Sunny upstairs and helped her into her Minnie Mouse printed pajamas. "Why did you go away Auntie?" she asked me drowsily, fighting off sleep with every breath. "Well," I said, calculating my words, "Do you remember when Uncle Aaron went to Heaven?"

She nodded and solemnly said, "I pray for him every night." I hugged her and said, "Well, when that happened, it was very hard for me to be where I had so many memories of him because I missed him so much. I needed to have a fresh start, especially with little Alba." She nodded solemnly and piped up again, "Does Alba miss Uncle Aaron?" I led her over to her bed and tucked the pink sheets around her, "Of course darling, but she has an amazing family that loves her very much. Now it's time to go to bed because your mommy won't be very happy if I keep you up. I love you!" I whispered. "I love you too," she murmured as her eyes fluttered shut. Her breathing steadied and I kissed her forehead as I stood to leave.

The next morning, I decided that I was going to go out and buy Christmas gifts for the girls and for Amelia. Alba and I caught a cab to the nearest mall. For Helena, a tomboyish ten year old, I bought a pair of blue and purple tie-dyed jeans, a chain necklace, a purple stuffed cat, and a purple shirt. For Avril, the definition of a girly-girl, I bought a long pink and white skirt, a necklace with pink beads, a pink stuffed puppy, and a pale rose long sleeved shirt with sparkles on it. And for Sunny, I bought a pink and gold dress with long sleeves, a set of pink bangles, a stuffed panda, and some headbands.

After that, I went to many different stores to shop for Amelia and bought a packet of cards and envelopes. By the end, I had bought her a new set of champagne glasses and a bottle of prosecco to go with them, a gorgeous set of thick metal bangles, a bright pink apron, and a pair of gold chandelier earrings. Then, I went into Carters to buy clothes for Mitch and Char's baby. I bought two outfits in lime green and yellow, which would look adorable on either a boy or a girl, and a stuffed giraffe with a bell on its neck. While there, I bought Alba a new shirt and pants with little ducks on them and a dress with a ladybug pattern and a matching headband that were for summer. For Mitch, I bought a sketchbook with soft, creamy pages and a set of acrylics. For Char, I bought a very modern, African styled golden necklace with black patterns and a matching bracelet.

Finally I shopped for the remaining members of my family: Stacy, John, Mom, and Dad. For Mom, I bought a red, silk scarf with delicate black birds stitched on it and a locket that I put a picture of Alba inside. For Stacy, I bought a gauzy, sky blue scarf with a cloudy white dye applied to it. For Dad, I bought a new, dark blue dress shirt and a tie with a striped black and white pattern. For John, I bought a fleecy pullover and a pair of grey sweatpants for his hikes.

I had all of the gifts wrapped at a stand set up by the local high school while I sat on a bench writing their cards from Alba and me. We went back to the house and I put Amelia and the girls' presents under the Christmas tree and packed the rest of the presents wherever they would fit in my suitcase and bag. The girls ran in the door, grinning and shouting snippets of their days before disappearing to do homework. I fed Alba again and sat playing with her on the floor. She crawled slowly away from me, giggling mischievously, her limbs tumbling over one another. Slowly, she pushed her hands against the ground and propelled herself upwards until she stood. "Alba! Good job!" I exclaimed. Her blue eyes widened in shock as she fell on her bottom again, then giggling again, she crawled into the haven of my lap.

That night when Amelia arrived home she said, "Well I see Santa has come early with Nicolette!" The girls ran to look under the tree and squealed at the names on each of their presents. Alba had woken up from her late afternoon nap and as we sat down in the living room, she was trying to imitate her standing success of earlier. When her legs buckled with the exertion, I sat her down on my lap and bounced her up and down on my knees. Avril crawled under the tree and grabbed various gifts, throwing them to her sisters. When she reached for her mother's gifts, I had to ask her not to throw them. Carefully obeying, she gently treaded over to her mom with each gift. Sunny was the first to tear open the wrapping paper of her panda and yelped with delight as she hugged it. Helena and Avril opened their packages that looked similar in shape. As the girls cuddled their stuffed animals close, I felt a wash of gratitude for the sweet refuge of childhood that still harbored them.

Next, they opened the bags with clothes and jewelry. Finally they opened the card with the note from me. They ran over, carefully minding Alba, and kissed me on the cheek, "Thank you Auntie!" After they sat back down, Amelia opened her gifts, exclaiming her thanks. The girls sat playing with their stuffed animals until Amelia told them it was time for bed and I put Alba in her crib. I went into each of their rooms, saying good night to Helena first and then Avril and Sunny. As I got ready for bed, I realized I was even more right than I had thought about coming to America; I saw the light in my eyes shone brighter and my heart weighed lighter.

On our last full day in San Francisco, Amelia, Sunny Avril, Helena, Alba, and I went out to Pier 39. We wandered around and with great delight, Avril, Sunny, and Helena went on the two-story carousel, carefully picking the most pristine, cheerful horses and tenderly stroking the chipped paint on the backs of others. After laughing at the wheezing and sluggishly sweet-eyed sea lions, we ambled through the cold winds drifting away from the sea and into a little candy store. Helena grabbed the most colorful candies, not bothering to read what they were. Sunny was a girl after my own heart, selecting a bag of various chocolates. Avril bought a bag of gummy bears, sour gummy worms, coke gummies, and Swedish fish. When we left, Helena popped a bright green colored candy in her mouth and then sticking out her tongue, cried, "Yuck." In order to make up for the suffering she had undergone, she stole one of Sunny's malt balls. Sunny burst into tears and pummeled Helena with her pint-sized fists. Avril stood by and laughed, cramming gummies into her mouth, as I rushed to hold back Sunny while Amelia grabbed Helena. We asked both of them to apologize and share happily and they glumly agreed.

We ate delicious curries and chicken at a Thai restaurant. When we arrived home, Amelia handed me a little box wrapped in golden ribbon. I beamed and opened it to find a gorgeous pair of earrings with long tendrils of metal coming down like the rays of the sun shining down. I embraced her and thanked her for the beautiful earrings and the wonderful stay with her family.

That night I dreamed of Aaron and myself in our New York condo. We first wandered into the kitchen over the course of the sun's long hours and danced to our favorite songs, both slow and fast paced. As darkness swirled around the rooms, filtering in through the windows and spreading like drops of dye into clear water, we danced into our bedroom. Aaron sat on the bed and pulled me into his lap where he kissed me and held me. The room swirled around us with the glint of a carousel, but we were still – the epicenter of the action. The sun rose as we entered the extra room. In the center of the pale pink room, there was a crib holding Alba. He picked her up and kissed her on the forehead. "I love you Alba, I love you Nicolette."

Three people paraded around me. My eyes flew open to find Sunny wrapped around my neck, Helena sitting on my legs and Avril standing behind me, belting a pop song at the top of her lungs. I laughed, untangling myself from the children, who possessed monkey-like agility, twisting themselves around me. "We don't want you to go!" screamed Sunny as Helena shouted, "Yeah, stay!" and Avril continued to sing. I grabbed them and wrapped them in a hug, planting a kiss on each of their heads. They giggled holding onto my neck and arms. After dressing and finishing our final packing, I kissed Amelia goodbye, slowly carrying Alba down the stairs. Amelia and the girls stood at the door, waving excitedly as I waved from the window of our taxi, blowing kisses to them.

Around eight in the morning, Alba and I boarded the airplane. Once Alba was calmly sitting on my lap, I turned on my iPad to watch Curious George without sound with Alba. She giggled at the colorful monkey's antics and the outraged expressions of the Man with the Yellow Hat. We arrived in New York and the flurry of excitement around us was contagious. I grabbed our suitcase off of the luggage carousel and hailed a taxi to my parents' apartment. Alba sat on my lap, staring out of the window at the glinting buildings of the city – no doubt in awe at the bright frenzy surrounding her. We drove past the Rockefeller Center and watched as little boys and girls tripped over their skates, experienced skaters glided easily backwards and forwards, and couples, old and young, held their dates close to them as they skated in sync. Alba pointed and stared out the window at the myriad new sights. I laughed, soaking in her enthusiasm, feeling the swift familiarity of home. We arrived at my parent's building and climbed the front steps.

Alba and I took the elevator up to their spacious, modern apartment on Central Park. Alba sat contently in her stroller as I knocked on the door. I heard the patter of my mother's soft feet as she rushed towards the door. The door opened a crack and then slid fully open as my mom's rosebud mouth opened and gasped, "Nicolette! Darling, it's so good to see you." I leaned down to her petite, French, five-foot-three form and hugged her close, "Hello Mama." A voice chirped from the other room, "Is she here?" My dad's long arms wrapped around me and held me, exclaiming how good it was to see me. I stepped away to find Mom kissing Alba's forehead and bouncing her up and down. I looked at my parents, standing side by side, and grinned. It had been so long since I had seen them in person and I soaked in every detail of their faces. First, my short, lovely, blonde mother with her lavender grey eyes and permanent smile and then my tall father. The complete female version of him, I had inherited his height, dark hair, slender form, and jade green eyes. They pulled me toward their guest room, my father wrapping his arm around me and my mother resting Alba on her hip. The circular bed was crisply made and the black curtains drawn away from the floor to ceiling windows. On the window, a sign draped, spelling, "Welcome home Nicolette!" Dropping my suitcase on the floor, I hugged them again, enveloping them both in my arms, thanking them for the warm welcome.

While I got ready to go to dinner, Mom took Alba in her arms. Turning on Christmas music, she danced with Alba, singing along in her dainty soprano voice. Resting a delicate hand on Alba's neck and another under her legs, she stepping around the living room, spinning and rocking her head back and forth. Whispering in her French-tinged English, she told Alba how much she had missed her, kissing her forehead with every word. Dad watched, a tender smile on his face, perhaps flitting back to the days when they were young parents, the house bustling with three children under the age of three, his own parents dancing through, making everything look a little easier. A tear traced his nose as he watched her dance, his green eyes soft with love. I wrapped my arms around him from behind, resting my head against his. He placed one hand over mine, "I love you my darling." I slipped around the couch and sat next to him, talking quietly and watching my mother and my daughter.

The spell was broken when the song came to an end and Mom looked up, grinning and asked if we would like to go to dinner. Set in the basement of a brick building with dim candles and softly glowing lights, the meal was delicious. Shadows shifted across the walls and created drifting splotches on our skin. The room was filled with our laughter as our voices joined together, then split again, excitedly detailing the last months of our lives. My mother's business was booming and my father's law firm was having one of its best years yet. Together, they were in the process of starting a program to help young entrepreneurs learn how to manage a business and gain the necessary skills. They asked about my life, inquiring about my alterations business and freelance writing, Alba's growth, and Leo. My head buzzed with the conversation, my smile tingling with the excitement of being back with my family.

The next morning, Alba sat on Dad's lap while Mom and I sipped coffee at the smooth black granite counter. Dad turned Alba to face him, peering into her blue eyes with his intent green ones. She blinked at him inquisitively and a booming laugh spread from his chest as he started to make faces at her. Mom hurried to the sink and I helped her wash the crumb-spattered porcelain plates and put them away. Reluctantly, Dad handed Alba to me and kissed me on the cheek, waiting for Mom to collect her briefcase. She kissed Alba and me on the cheek and promised that after the next two days, she and Dad would be taking time off to spend with us. I waved as they stepped outside hand in hand and strolled to the elevator.

Balancing Alba on my hip, I wandered to the windows in the lounge. The spiny skeletons of trees poked up from Central Park, jostling one another with their thin arms, prodded by the winds. They stood tall from the spotted center of a sheet-rippled pond. Boulders climbed over one another, tumbling to create mini mountains. An orange coated speckle of a child stood on top of the pile of rocks, the lone victor of a struggle only he would know, a hero of an epic in his mind. Plumes of smoke floated away from the vendors on the streets as languidly as the first notes of an orchestra. The gray crisscrossing streets swarmed with the scurrying beehive of people, flying with their might against the currents of wind. The clouds in the sky dropped like the curtain of a stage set, obscuring the metallic buildings and veiling the city in that familiar, exotic veneer.

Alba and I wandered down the street to Char and Mitch's apartment and rung the bell to be let up. After climbing the stairs to the door and knocking, a very heavily pregnant Char opened the door drowsily. Her eyes gleaming the minute she saw who was at the door. "Nicolette!" she cried and tugged me into her arms. Mitch tumbled down the stairs and tackled me with a hug. He put his arm around me and we followed Char into their living room. Char and Mitch's very enthusiastic dog, Shadow, almost knocked me over with his force as he jumped up, licking my face.

We sat down around the table, the room congested with the thrill of being together. Our words fluttered into the air quickly, tumbling over each other. Char took Alba in her lap, bouncing her up and down, asking me questions about my own pregnancy and Alba's birth. Her voice was fraught with anticipation, quivering on a tightrope of emotions running the full gamut of emotions from jubilation to glee to fear. She stretched as she yawned, pouring her emotions out with each breath. When we had spoken for hours and her voice ran ragged with exertion and tiredness, I kissed Char on the cheek and told her to rest.

As Alba and I ambled down the street, I marveled once more at the fusion and intermingling of shining modern towers and classical architecture. I smiled at the thought that I now lived in a place a world away from here, yet the same sights still struck me: the tourists and rushing cars, the young and old mixed together busily going about life, the marvelous architecture, the rushing fountains, and everything in a constant state of construction and change. We walked around Midtown and I held Alba to me as we wandered, her blue eyes bright with the reflections of the starry buildings. Her head flopped forward and her eyes became droopy as she fell asleep on my shoulder. I walked slowly back to Mom and Dad's apartment and I lay down on the bed after placing Alba in a Pack 'n Play Mom had found, drifting off to sleep with the sweet sound of her breath.

The next day, I pushed Alba's stroller through the rushing streets, going to Stacy and John's apartment after calling them to make sure they were home. Christmas lights blinked busily across doorways and through windows, wrapped around pillars and adorning tree trunks. Jingling from the Santa-hat suited Salvation Army bell ringers rang through the streets, accompanied by a cheerful "Good morning." Rich choir voices chanted in the streets, mouths wide in song, arms spread in exultation, robes dripping from their bodies and swirling in the wind. Verdant wreaths sprouted from doorways and shop windows, Poinsettias bloomed from window boxes, greeting the cold jauntily. We found our way to their beautiful apartment in Tribeca. I knocked on the door and John opened it with a grin, exclaiming our names and pulling us into the apartment. Stacy ran to the door at the sound of the commotion, "We've been expecting you!" She whipped Alba out of her stroller and hugged her tightly. John spun me around in a hug, "It is so good to see you." John took Alba from Stacy and he lifted her into the air, making her giggle, while Stacy put her arm around me.

We sat in their living room that looked out onto the red ribbon wrapped fire escape and I pulled out their gifts from underneath Alba's stroller. Wishing them a Merry Christmas, I handed Stacy and John their festively ribbon draped gifts. Thanking me and kissing me on the cheek, Stacy hurried off and returned with a deep blue box. I stripped away the crisp layers of tissue paper to reveal the heart of the box, an album. "I made a scrapbook of Aaron when I was deep in my sorrow of losing him. It's some of the memories I have of him and you, and of your life together. I want you to have it," she choked. My heart sped up and my breath grew more ragged. I hugged her close, "Thank you, thank you, thank you." She collapsed next to me on the couch with a little smile, holding my hand as

John bounced Alba on his lap with his boundless enthusiasm. I always thought that Aaron was most like him. Aaron was so bright and lively; he and I had balanced one another so well.

We stayed with Stacy and John for about an hour more, promising to meet for lunch later during the week. After that, I carefully placed my wrapped scrapbook in the bottom of the stroller and pushed Alba back to Mom and Dad's apartment for her nap.

I decided that Alba and I would visit the cemetery where Aaron was buried later that afternoon. After stopping at a nearby bodega, we caught a cab, a bouquet of roses in the crook of my right arm and Alba in my left arm. I gingerly stepped over the icy paths to Aaron's grave and knelt in the snow beside it. I touched the headstone with butterfly fingers, tracing his name slowly. Alba watched me intently, "Mama?" I sat down on the ground, placing Alba in my lap. She wrapped her arms around my neck and I rocked back and forth with her in my arms, pressing my chin to her head, and told Alba a story.

"Once upon a time, there was a princess who fell in love with the most amazing prince in the world. As the days, months, and years passed, he fell in love with her. They courted and were happier than anyone could have imagined. He carried her away and they married. The princess and the prince were the rulers of a small and beautiful world. They passed though happiness and sadness together, arm in arm with twinkles in their eyes. One day, the princess found out she was going to have a baby and they rejoiced. But the bliss could not carry on so; the sky was torn open and pulled the prince away from the princess, to a wonderful place, Heaven, where the sun always shines and people are always happy. The princess's sadness enveloped her, a darkness spreading across the land. But a spark grew in her heart with the baby inside of her. That spark lit a candle of discovery. The four winds carried the princess beyond her homeland to a magical land beyond the sea where she gave birth to the baby, a beautiful little girl. They were happy in the magical foreign land and the baby grew as lovely as the sun. The princess and her baby went back to their kingdom to see those they loved. The darkness slowly faded away until there was only love. And as the princess and her daughter looked out over the frosted land of her kingdom, the prince's life was remembered and they would never forget him. He floated, perched above them, watching them with a smile, guiding them through their lives, carried always in their hearts. Soon the princess and her daughter will return to the land beyond the sea but neither this land nor the prince will ever be forgotten."

Alba clapped her hands at my story and I looked at Aaron's grave. "This is where your father is buried, Alba. But he lives in Heaven now and is carried with us always in our hearts. He was gentle and kind. He loved to laugh and joke and he brought joy wherever he went." My voice choked, "You have the same eyes as him, Alba. They were bright blue and shone like the glimmer of sun on the Adriatic. He loves you so very much Alba." I laid the roses against the headstone and whispered, "I love you Aaron, thank you for our time together." I sat there with Alba and the memory of Aaron and wished again and again that he could be there with our baby and with me.

My parents' vacation started the next day. Wrapped in our coats, we journeyed into the cold, strolling to Le Pain Quotidien. We sat in a warmth-drenched corner, coats draped across the back of pale wooden chairs, ordering crisp Belgian Waffles with cascading mountains of strawberries and soft snows of powdered sugar and hot chocolate. The chocolate arrived in a small silver pitcher, the milk frothed in a separate cup. We poured the chocolate in with a flourish, the sweet warmth bubbling up, slowly turning the milk's purity to hazy brown seductiveness. The Belgian Waffles were no less of a marvel, with hazelnut chocolate spread lavishly smoothed across the valleys and hills of the waffles, dancing in flavor with the tart pop of strawberry. Filled with the emanating heat of the meal, we ambled onto the streets and into Central Park, the clipped sound of hooves on the pavement smacking in the near distance and the soft rumble of voices permeating the chill. Children grinned as they slipped across the ice skating rink, feet tumbling over one another, hands hitting the ground in defeat, followed by jubilation of recovery and movement again.

The following days passed similarly to the first, with pleasant jaunts through the city and delicious meals with family and friends. I spoke with Leo on most of those peaceful days spent with my family in my old home. We had long conversations and talked of the rush of the holidays in both Italy and America. Leo was visiting Milan to see his parents. He had told them about me and they could not wait to meet Alba and me. Alba recognized him in the spotty picture on my screen and would wave and wave.

As the baby's due date approached, Alba and I went to sit with Char. We relaxed, drinking hot chocolate and chatting as Alba practiced crawling around the room. Around lunchtime, Char asked me to pick up her favorite Thai curry from a local restaurant while she rested. I walked down the street to the restaurant with Alba in a stroller and lingered inside the restaurant among bamboo stalks and tinkling waterfalls, the fragrant spices of the curries tantalizing. With the crinkling Styrofoam cartons of rice and curry carefully nestled in the compartment of Alba's stroller, we walked back, surrounded by the hazy glow of streetlights radiating in the dark evening.

The next morning, Mom, Alba, and I went out into the streets where vibrant garlands glimmered on door fronts; romantically melting candles flickered from windows; and Christmas trees sprouted from mountains of cloth in storefront displays. The sky shone clear blue with transient wisps of clouds. The fragrant scent of macaroons beckoned from a small storefront. Saccharine, richly colored, melting – grandiose bows festooned the two golden boxes that we purchased.

Back on the streets, with scarves draping our necks and breath crystalizing in the air, we stepped down the stairs to watch the skaters glide around Rockefeller rink. Prometheus gleamed, his garments flowing in the breeze that carried him and picked us up to pull us back through time, to a time of the joy and simplicity of togetherness that filled the air during Christmas. Laughing breathlessly at memories and talking excitedly about the future, I saw the light of life, which sometimes seems snuffed, burn as brightly as ever.

Early in the morning on Christmas Eve, the ring of the telephone resounded through the apartment. Drowsily, I stretched and reached for the phone next to my bed and yawned, "Hello?" Mitch's frantic voice sounded, "Nicolette, the baby is coming. Char's water broke." Char's voice murmured in the background and Mitch spoke again, "She wants you to meet us at the hospital. Please tell Mom and Dad."

I knocked on Mom and Dad's door, excitedly calling their names. Mom peeped out the door curiously as I told her that Char's water had broken and the baby was coming. Her mouth spread in a grin, "Michael get dressed, we're going to the hospital." We dressed hastily and tumbled out the door, Alba perched on my hip, and flagged a cab.

In hushed voices, we eagerly talked about the baby's coming.

Mitch and Char's baby was born by mid-morning; Mitch called us into the room once the baby was cleaned up. Char sat holding their baby boy, who was wrapped in blue blankets and had a soft golden patch of hair on the top of his head. She spoke softly for the first time since I had met her, "Meet Sean Aaron Thompson." When I heard Aaron's name, my mouth spread in an even wider smile and my eyes brimmed with tears, "Oh Char, he's beautiful." She smiled serenely and said, "Thanks Nicolette, I'm so glad that you're here to meet him. Will you be his godmother?" I leaned down and kissed her cheek.

Mom and Dad sat talking to Mitch and Char and I brought Alba to see Sean. She looked down at him, tilting her head. She reached down to touch his head and I gently bent over so that she could get a clearer look at him. Quietly, I introduced her to him, "Alba, this is your cousin, Sean." She giggled and said, "Hi." Char smiled, holding Sean close to her and kissing his brow. I watched Char's pale eyes move gently over her son, taking him in, finally seeing and feeling the miracle she had carried to life.

When Alba and I returned to my parents' apartment, I placed the gifts for my mom and dad under the chic evergreen tree: shiny silver ribbons darting around it and glowing ornaments both magnifying the dancing ceiling lights and reflecting the dim glow of the city. Mom hurried around the kitchen singing Christmas songs and swaying her head as she danced from fridge to sink to counter. My eyes crinkled with a smile, "I love you Mom." She looked up, her feet still dancing, "What was that Nicolette?" "Thank you for everything Mom, I love you." She danced over to me, "I love you too my darling daughter," and pulled me with her as her dance turned into a frenzied jitterbug. I laughed and laughed, and as Dad walked into the apartment and pulled Mom to him in a dramatic tango finished with a kiss under the mistletoe of a ceiling light, I could not have been more grateful for our lives and all of the love that surrounded us.

As we sat around the Christmas tree with full stomachs, Mom's face lit up with excitement. She held out a silver box towards me, "Nicolette, you'll never guess what I was able to get you!" Mom crowed. Dad's face lit up as he bragged, "She told me what it was! You're going to love it."

I laughed as they watched animatedly, trying to give me hints or telling me just how exciting it was. Grinning, I tore the paper gingerly and opened the box to find a room card for room 803, a junior executive suite, at Trump International Hotel and Tower, Central Park, for December 31st. I hugged both of them, excitedly asking how on earth she had gotten a room there on such short notice. She winked and wrinkled her nose at me jokingly, "That's for me to know." Then she stated the rest of the gift, "That day and night, your dad and I will look after Alba so that you are free to do whatever you wish." I gave her a hug, "Thank you so much!" She shook her head and told me they absolutely could not wait to spend time with their grandbaby!

Alba clapped her hands as her grandma picked her up and handed her a pink wrapped present. Alba threw the paper in the air and tried to catch it as I took out a stacking toy, a stuffed elephant, and a blue and purple ruffled dress. "Say 'grazie' to granny!" I told her. "Grat-zee," she cooed. I tickled her and she giggled. Mom smiled at us as I played with Alba, "I always knew you would be a wonderful mother Nicolette." I grinned at her, "Only because I learned from the best." I paused and then ruefully wondered, "Should I have moved to Italy? I just feel like I don't see you enough and I'm depriving you of the chance to see Alba." She took my hands in her hands and looked me in the eye, "Never, ever second guess yourself on what you did. You did the best, most right thing you could have done in your situation. I can see that you are very happy there and that makes us happy. And you can always come back any time you like!"

The next morning, we put Alba in her stroller and put on our coats to take Alba to the Central Park Zoo. Stacy and John met us there. We chatted animatedly as we sauntered through the park, the jungle-like sheets of evergreen trees obscuring what surprises lay around the next bend. Alba adored watching the penguins zip through the icy blue water, propelled flawlessly as if by motor. Upon seeing the monkeys, she shouted, "George!" and watched her favorite character in action, swinging across rope swings and climbing towers, mischievously leaping to taunt their friends with tugs to the fur. We visited the children's part of the zoo, watching the metal animals on the clock tower parade in a circle with bittersweet metal clangs. Alba petted a llama, smiling broadly as she shyly placed her small hand on the llama's downy fur.

We left the zoo, stepping into "Le Pain" for mugs of hot chocolate to release the bitter cold. After returning to the warm apartment, I opened Stacy's scrapbook and slowly soaked in each page as the memories washed over me. There were pictures of Aaron and me from our high school years: prom, graduation, dances, Central Park, summer vacations, followed by college and then our wedding. The changes in our faces – changes I had barely noticed as time passed – struck me as I watched the two of us grow up together. I stared at us in front of our apartment, taking in every detail and expression of us standing with our arms wrapped around each other. Another showed us painting together in Washington Square. Finally, there was a series of pictures of Aaron and me in India, Australia, and Morocco on mission trips, exploration trips, and hiking trips. The pictures in India were brightest, the most recent, with me wrapped in a sun-gold sari, a golden veil perched on my dark curls, and a sparkling gem on my forehead while Aaron sported an orange shirt with red embroidery, his blonde hair stark against the dark-haired masses around us. In another photo, we sat in the orphanage where we volunteered with the grinning little girls and mischievous boys, first lost in their shyness when we arrived, then clinging in their love for us when we left. In Australia, Aaron and I sat on a boat, wrapped in diving suits and covered in gear, the crystal clear waters around us, the sun low on the horizon, its image mirrored in the ripples. Another picture showed us surrounded by bamboo stalks, koalas clinging to our shoulders with their mouths half-open in the process of chewing eucalyptus leaves, at the Lone Pine Koala Sanctuary near Brisbane. In Morocco, our faces shone pink with the exertion of hiking in the High Atlas Mountains. The red undulation of the mountains curved around us, the green smatterings of grasses and barren trees splattered across the landscape. Our backpacks, stacked high and covered in a pale red dust, perched stoically on our backs as the trail behind us stretched to eternity. On the second to last page was a picture of Alba and me in the Boboli Gardens, her blue eyes staring through the camera. The last page read, "You are loved."

Chapter Fifteen

On New Year's Eve, I told Mom and Dad that I planned to ring in the New Year at Times Square. My phone rang, "Ciao Nicolette!" said Marina's fuzzy voice and then followed with a barrage of questions, "How are you? What is America like? What are you doing for the New Year?" I answered how good it was to hear from her and we enjoyed catching up. I told her how New York City was as wonderful as ever, and that I was passing the last of the old year in Times Square. My parents watched me with pride in their eyes as I spoke in rapid Italian. Marina told me that her parents were coming back to Florence with her that day and they were going to have a little party at her apartment. We hung up after cheerful goodbyes and wishes for a happy new years celebration. I excused myself from Mom and Dad and slipped into black jeans, olive green combat boots, a black sweater, and my coat, finishing the ensemble by looping a green scarf around my neck. After dressing, I packed a little overnight bag with black-and-white polka-dotted pajamas and a long-sleeved short black dress with a pair of tights for the next day. I filled my purse with two or three granola bars and a water bottle. I told my parents that I was going to drop off my bag at Trump then go to Times Square. In the middle of the afternoon, I kissed Alba and my parents goodbye, thanked them, and made my way off alone into the city – something I had not done for almost a year. The energy of New York drew me, practically pulling me with the vibration of its people and the static excitement for the year gone by and anticipation of the New Year to come.

I strolled down the street, my bag swinging from one arm, to Trump International on Central Park. After checking in, I stepped into the gilded elevator, my reflection glinting around me. I strolled into my room and stopped, spinning around as I looked at the plush bed and beautifully modern design of the room. I dropped my bag and walked back downstairs and into the cold. My leisurely gait slowed as I looked behind me, hearing footsteps pounding on the sidewalk. "Nicolette!" a voice resounded. Suddenly Leo stood aside me, his arms held wide open. "Oh my God," I exclaimed. He pulled me towards him and I buried my head in his chest, my voice muffled against his coat, "What are you doing here?" He calmly replied, "I figured that we might as well spend our first New Year together and I missed you." I laughed as he wrapped his arms around me and I murmured in Italian, "But how?" "Your Mama told me!" I laughed pulling away from him and looking into his eyes, "I've missed you." His familiar brown eyes crinkled with the smile that played on his lips and he touched my cheek, "I never want to be apart for this long again."

After dropping his small duffle bag back at the hotel, we walked the short distance to Times

Square and found our way through the crowds until we were pressed against a front barrier. Out of every single person there, we found ourselves next to a Florentine. Her name was Kirsten and her family had emigrated from Sweden to Italy when she was a toddler. She was here with her fiancée, an American, named Tommy. We began chatting instantly, talking about Florence, her upcoming wedding, and my baby. Tommy laughed at us as we spoke our spitfire Italian and talked to Leo in English.

We soon switched to English to include Tommy in the conversation. The two of them were going to move to Florence and were to be married in the Duomo in June. Before we knew it, Leo and I found ourselves invited to the wedding.

The hours passed amiably with our new friends. Concerts played and music boomed through loudspeakers. The crowds sang along rowdily, the excitement passing from one person to the next, pressed between every jacket, fluttering with the snow. The hours sped by, the crowds growing anxious for midnight's excitement. As the temperature dropped steadily, I wrapped my scarf around my nose and mouth and pulled a black knit hat out of my bag. Leo slung his arm across my shoulder and I leaned my head against his shoulder. Kirsten cuddled closer to Tommy and he wrapped his arms around her, whispering something in her ear.

The clock ticked and ticked closer to midnight until it was one minute to twelve. The crowd joined the countdown and Leo and I grinned at each other as the glowing ball slid down the building. With one voice, the masses counted down until at the split second's silence of zero; we erupted. With the New Year's cheers, flashing lights, and falling confetti, Leo dipped me back in his arms like couples had once done in a spot quite nearby at the end of World War II. The familiar strains of Auld Lang Syne floated by and we held each other. Fluffy flakes of snow stuck to our heads as we swayed back and forth, smiling at the clean slate of a New Year. "I love you Nicolette, more than I thought I ever could love anyone." I pressed my lips to his and then pulled away and grinned, "I love you too." Out of the corner of my eye, I glanced at Tommy and Kirsten, who were hugging next to us. I soaked in every precious second, every precious detail, the fluorescent lights of the advertisements and blinking repetition, "Happy New Year, Happy New Year," the soft pelt of confetti on our shoulders, and the light pressure of Leo's coat against mine. The song ended and we started dancing to the more upbeat music that followed.

Kirsten and I made sure that we had each other's phone numbers and hugged goodbye. Then, Leo put one arm around my shoulder and took my hand in his other one. We pushed our way through the crowds until finally we were able to walk freely.

We walked into the elevator at Trump, listening to the quiet whir of the motor and the hum of music playing in the background. We quietly trod down the hallway and into the room. I slipped into the bathroom to dress in my pajamas and came out to find Leo in dark blue flannel pajamas, sitting on the bed, flipping through a book on New York, absorbed in a picture of Central Park in summer. I slid under the covers and sat amidst the piles of pillows. He slipped into the bed next to me and wrapped his arms around me. I rested my head against him and kissed him slowly. His hands drifted across my face, stroking my hair. Whispering a goodnight, I pulled away, still smiling and fell asleep. In a breath of a word, Leo murmured, "Goodnight my Nicolette."

I woke up at ten the next morning to find Leo kissing my jawline. I put my arms around his neck and he pulled me closer. We spoke about our holidays and laughed together at the simple pleasure of being together once more. I remained in his embrace, resting my head on his shoulder and taking in his face, his strong jaw and aristocratic nose, his brilliant eyes and the dark hair pushed back on his head. I kissed him on the tip of his nose and got out of the bed to dress and get ready. After we had packed our small bags, Leo slid my coat over my arms and pulled his leather jacket tightly shut. We took the elevator down to check out of the hotel.

We strolled down the streets, a slight hangover of the celebration seemed to hover in the air, the sun's prodding alarm forcing the city upwards and outwards. Horns blared in the street and young people slunk into restaurants to sip a Bloody Mary or two. The artists yawned as they set up their wares: caricatures of celebrities, vintage signs, chalk drawings, spray painted pieces of metal, glimmering landscapes and hazy cityscapes. My mom and dad opened the door of their apartment, practically glowing. "Alba was so good! And hello again Leo!" I laughed and exclaimed, "Last night was fantastic Mom, thank you so much! And thank you for telling Leo where I was." Alba looked up in awe and exclaimed, "Leo!" He picked her up and kissed her head, "Alba!" She patted his face and I laughed as he kissed her head once more.

We decided to go out and simply absorb every last bit of sunshine and wind. Leo was impressed by the architecture and sheer height of the buildings. Alba waved at every person we passed. The drowsiness burned off with the speed of fog on a sunny morning, and soon the streets bustled with their typical strength and buzz once more. The shutter of Mom's camera blinked as she snapped photos, bringing the day to life for future days. Venturing through the winding streets of boutique shops and bohemian clothing, we climbed up the stairs to the High Line as the sun set. The peachy pinks of sunset swept across the skyline, cut into by the wispy limbs of trees climbing into the air. The buildings shook with the sunlight, each glass window a mirror for the sun to vainly peek at her beauty. Pale white wisps of cloud slowly imbibed the colors around them until they were wound into fair cotton candy strips. Shadows of people moved along with us, all of us fish propelled by the waves of wind across a sea floor of planks and metal.

Leo managed to purchase a seat on the plane that was quite near mine. Alba and I exchanged tearful goodbyes with my parents and they promised to visit again soon and to text and call often. Then Leo, Alba, and I hopped into a taxi to the airport. We sat in the gate area for our flight to Milan. Alba watched the planes taking off in awe, their long arms glinting in the evening light. A single student sitting next to Alba and me traded seats with Leo so that he could sit next to us. As the hours of the flight passed, I fed Alba a bottle of formula and walked up and down the aisles holding her until she was asleep. It was an overnight flight and Leo and I passed Alba between us so that we could both get some sleep.

Arriving back in Florence, soft sleep carried Alba and me away into a foggy, jet-lagged haze.

The next day, Leo met us to go for a short walk and helped us pick up some groceries, meandering through the aisles of vegetables that gleamed under the moisture and light of their temporary home and through the milky pale parted waves of cheeses. The distinctive, unmistakable smell of Italian espresso saturated the air around us. Smiling, I asked Leo how on Earth he had come up with the idea to suddenly fly to New York and find us. He simply replied, "I had to see you; you were worth the trip."

Chapter Sixteen

Early in January, Leo arrived at my apartment and swept me off my feet in a hug. "Darling, I want you to meet my parents." I grinned, "Fantastic, when are we going?" He responded, "Well, I made a reservation at L'Osteria Di Giovanni for dinner at 7:30 tonight. Marina agreed to watch Alba for tonight." He caressed my cheek, "They will love you just as much as I do."

With Alba on my hip, I walked down the hall that night to meet Leo and his parents at Marina's apartment. I knocked on the door and Leo came to my side, "Mama, Papa, this is Nicolette. Nicolette, this is my mother, Arabella, and my father, Francesco." "It's a pleasure to meet you," I smiled and then gesturing to Alba, said, "This is my daughter, Alba." Francesco waved at her and Arabella smiled, "Hello Nicolette, hello little Alba." Francesco stood tall with a lightly wrinkled face with smiling eyes. Arabella's eyes were kind and light brown. Marina came out to pick up Alba and I kissed Alba on the forehead and hugged Marina.

The four of us walked over the icy cobblestones. Few tourists wandered the streets, leaving the city quiet and peaceful. We walked along the riverside, making small talk and avoiding swirling puddles and piles of snow and slush.

The waiter poured Prosecco with an expert hand, allowing not a drop to escape the thin confines of the glass. The liquid bubbled up, lighthearted and carefree. Francesco lifted his glass, "To meeting Nicolette." I raised my glass and smiled at him, "To meeting Leo's wonderful parents." The twinkling glasses caught the light as they clinked together, resounding with a classy note.

The meal passed happily with non-stop conversation and laughter. Francesco was kind and quiet-spoken, but always ready with a hearty laugh. Arabella on the other hand was very talkative and welcoming. She grinned and asked about Alba, talking about Marina and Leo as children and of their grandchildren. We walked out of the restaurant later deliciously full. Leo took my hand and squeezed it. Outside their hotel, Arabella kissed me on both cheeks, "I am so glad to have met you my dear." I smiled, "It was lovely to meet you too." Francesco gave me a hug and said, "You are a darling. Leo should count his blessings." I kissed his worn cheek.

The coldest time of the year passed over Florence during January and February, leaving cold blankets of snow over Florence's waiting, arched back. Alba and I stayed inside unless we absolutely needed to go out. The business for my sewing flowed steadily, bringing in new coats to be taken in and old dresses to be let out, scarves with runs and pants with holes. My business began to expand to creation and design, in addition to mending and sizing; challenging and fun, I enjoyed the process of designing and creating garments designed and fitted to precise perfection.

Thick white slabs of snow sat like marble on the balcony, prime for carving yet too pure to disturb. Dots of snow obscured the view, dripping from frozen to *semifreddo*. The fire burned, slowly breaking down logs, pale orange heat wavering and bounding across the room. Leo came to dinner most nights, sitting with Alba and me, absorbing the warmth that danced across the room, suavely picking up the cold and lifting it back into the air.

Alba's first birthday was on April third. On the first of April, when Leo came over for dinner, he excitedly picked up Alba and said to me, "It is Alba's birthday in two days, isn't it?" As I nodded, Leo asked, "Then how would you like to go on a little vacation?" I grinned as he pulled out a set of train tickets and told me that he was taking three days off work to take us to Cinque Terre for Alba's birthday. He ruffled Alba's dark curls and kissed her forehead as we strolled into the living room. I kissed Leo, thanking him and asking him about what to pack and what Cinque Terre was like.

Leo knocked on my door the next morning with a broad smile and helped carry down Alba's stroller and our suitcase. We arrived at the station via taxi, boarded the train, and found our spacious compartment for six people. The gray surfaces of other trains disappeared behind us as the bullet like front of our train pierced the countryside. Bright yellow flowers bloomed in the fields and puddles of rainwater and melted snow pooled along the sides. Lone cows stood, staring at the metallic beast plowing past them, and then with a blasé flick of their tail, turned around and sauntered off.

When the first signs of the azure water and stunning cliffs appeared, I gasped. Pastel buildings blossomed from the rocky cliffs, gaping black-eyed windows staring from them. Boats bobbed merrily in the harbor, floating aside red buoys. Pinstriped umbrellas budded from sand like the swirled lollipops of youth. The water crashed against the rocks with an exaggerated slap, laughing with the giggle of a gull. Alba rested her hands against the glass from where she was sitting on my lap, her hands creating transient imprints on the window. We stepped out of the train onto a small platform at Monterosso, one of the five towns that make up Cinque Terre, and pulled our bags to the hotel where we were staying. The salt hung in the air, fresh and impertinent, stinging the eyes and clearing the lungs.

It was still early in the day, so I changed into a bikini and dressed Alba in a pink polka-dotted swimsuit and strapped a pink and white hat onto her head. I covered Alba in baby sunscreen. When I came out with a black dress over my swimsuit and Alba on my hip, Leo stood waiting, already dressed and beckoned with a grin. We found an outdoor restaurant that hovered on the edge of the stone beach; the tables sat, shadowed by umbrellas that flapped in the wind. Leo and I shared a salad and fantastic pesto gnocchi. We smiled at the taste of the melting potato pasta and creamy pesto as it disappeared from the plate, one delicate piece at a time.

Leo and I sat at a spot where the breeze flowed beautifully across the nearly empty, pebbly beach. The sun-warmed ground burned the soles of my feet. I pulled off my cover-up and Leo took off his t-shirt. Alba sat contently on a blanket we had laid out and reached for a fistful of sand. Then she stood up, a look of immense concentration hovering on her face, and took a step. And then another one. I grinned as I grabbed my phone and started to take a video. She took another step, and then fell on her behind. I picked her up and lifted her in the air, "Good job Alba!" Leo laughed, "I can't believe it!" She struggled to get down and then she stood again and took another step and fell. Giggling, she crawled back to me. I kissed her on the head and she giggled. I carried her to the ocean and she stuck a foot out into the water and recoiled. I walked in up to my ankles and dipped her little feet into the water and this time she giggled; I dipped her in again and again until she stood in the water by herself, holding my hands.

Leo ran in, picking her up and spinning her around in the air, little droplets of water flying from her feet like a sprinkler. She giggled even more and Leo put her back in the shallow water, where she promptly fell down with a little explosion of water around her. She sat amidst the water and splashed her hands up and down, making momentary crevices in the surf. Alba giggled with excitement.

Leo put Alba down on the beach blanket and picked me up instead. He spun me around, holding my waist and then kissed me. I laughed as he put me down and kissed his cheek, "Thank you Leo, for everything you've done for us."

I lay down on the blanket next to Alba, who was playing with sand. Alba threw the grains in the air like confetti and squealed, "Yay!" She clapped enthusiastically. Leo sat with her and I lay down, letting the sun's rays beat down on my flesh and the breeze course across my body. Alba climbed onto my stomach and I cuddled her closely and wrapped her in a towel with me. Leo took my hand, "I'm so glad that we could come on this vacation, it's good to escape the city life for a while isn't it?" I smiled. "I'll take that as a yes," he grinned. Pieces of sand lunged across the beach, drifting among the pebbles, helpless at the hands of the breeze. Leo played with a pebble, tossing it into the air and catching it, looking out pensively at the ocean. His back rippled as he stretched with a yawn. Alba's mouth opened in a yawn also, her eyes drowsy. Slowly, languid from the sun, we stood and packed the blanket, and with Alba snuggled against my chest, we went into the hotel.

Once in the bathroom, I stripped off Alba's swimsuit, wrapping her in a towel and threw our sandy suits in a sink full of water. After wrapping myself in a robe, I let about half a foot of lukewarm water run into the bathtub. I held Alba, sheathed in her towel blanket and sang songs to her while waiting for the water. I dipped a hand in to test the water temperature and once approving, placed Alba in the tub. She splashed and I gently poured water over her head, running my hand through her curls to remove the traces of sand and sea. I swaddled Alba in a towel and then went into the room to put her diaper on. I asked Leo to put her down for an afternoon nap.

When the bathtub was nearly full of lovely, steaming water, I stepped in and shivered with delight at the perfection. I sunk in and let the water loosen tensions in my body. I scrubbed the sand off my skin and out of my hair and thought back on the perfect day. When my skin was rubbed to a bright shade of pink and my soaked hair was dripping down the curve of my shoulders, I decided to get out. I wrapped my hair into a turban with a towel, draped my robe around me, lightly tying it, and then wrung out our swimsuits and hung them over the shower rod. I found Leo lying on the bed next to Alba; he was sleeping on top of the blankets in a robe like mine. His arm was protectively around Alba and the worries of life that were so plainly written on his face during the day had lessened to make his the face peacefully angelic. A soft smile found its way onto my face.

I slipped out of my robe and took my hair out of the turban and quickly pulled on a bra, panties, and a strapless, long dark blue dress with a slit up the side, and Leo stirred as I adjusted the dress's waist and neckline. His dark eyelashes fluttered open, revealing his even darker eyes, and he smiled at me. "Hello my angel," he whispered. I grinned and my short hair fell in front of my face. He gently took his arm out from under Alba and stood. He wrapped his arms around me, tucked away my stray curls, and kissed me softly. "Mr. Caviatolli, you just made my knees go weak." He laughed – a bold, happy sound, and grinned, "I'm glad." He walked into the bathroom. I heard the shower turn on and lay down next to Alba, who had woken up and was starting to stretch.

After changing her diaper, I put Alba back into her dress from earlier that day. Leo came out of the bathroom in jeans and a button down blue dress shirt. He pulled on a sports jacket and I dressed Alba in a sweater and put on a cropped cotton jacket. I picked up Alba and Leo took my right hand. We walked down to the hotel restaurant, a fancy café with a specialty of seafood. Alba was treated like a princess and given chickpeas and a purée of fresh pear. I ordered an arugula salad dressed with walnuts, pears, and grilled vegetables while Leo ordered swordfish with citron dressing. It was fantastic and all three of us enjoyed every bite of it.

We walked back to our room, exhausted from the sunshine and sting of salt in our eyes. I put Alba into pajamas and I pulled on black cotton pants and a grey tank top. I placed Alba into a spare baby cot from the hotel and waited until I heard her soft breathing. Leo unbuttoned his shirt and pulled on a t-shirt over it. He walked over to where I was perched on the bed, kissed my forehead, and whispered, "Sleep well Nicolette." I whispered back, "I love you." "Love you too." He kissed me on the forehead, "Get some rest."

At five a.m. Alba started to cry and I woke up. I picked her up and rocked her back and forth and bounced her up and down, "Happy birthday Alba!" She quieted down and her usual smile spread across her angelic face. Leo lay asleep amidst the covers. I scribbled a quick note on a scrap of paper and put it on the bedside table, tugged a windbreaker over my tank top, and wrapped Alba in a sweater. After strapping her into her stroller, I quietly closed the door behind us.

There was a path just above the beach where the sea winds pushed and pulled and the earth's heartbeat seemed ever closer. My hair whipped across my face and the salty, moist breeze wove its way into my clothes. The sun began her journey into the sky and as her light rays flashed across the dewy face of the sky, they illuminated Alba's bright face and even brighter future.

When Alba and I went back to the room, I found Leo making the bed. "You're back," he smiled and then took Alba out of the stroller where she was dozing again and cried, "Happy first birthday!" She woke up and I held my breath, hoping she wouldn't start to cry. I let out a deep breath as she clapped her hands and said, "Le-oh." He grinned proudly, "Why don't we go for breakfast?" "Why don't we change first?" I laughed. Leo, already dressed in swimming shorts with jeans over them and a t-shirt, sat patiently while Alba and I put on swimsuits and cover-ups.

We ate a fresh breakfast of fruit and granola and picked up towels from the front desk. Alba crawled and toddled up and down the beach with Leo holding her left hand and me holding her right when she managed to walk. When her dimpled legs were too tired to continue, she and I sat down on a towel and Leo went to purchase some drinks.

He came back with two bottles of water, a chocolate bar, an Italian fashion magazine for me, a newspaper for him, and a coloring book for Alba. I flipped through the pages of the magazine and Alba scribbled around and across pictures of Disney fairies. She held the book towards me and I extolled praise on her Picasso-esque masterpiece. We turned the page for Alba and she wrinkled her brow in concentration as she worked. When we were all hot and sweating from the sun, I helped Alba up and we ambled toward the sea.

After splashing around and playing in the water with Alba while Leo took many pictures, we went back into the hotel and I gave Alba her bath. I put aloe on my reddened nose and showered. At dinner, Alba was given a birthday candle in a dish of gelato. The waiter took a picture of Leo, Alba, and me, and said, "You're a beautiful family; I wish you the best always." Touched, we thanked him. Leo and I helped to blow out the candle. I let the gelato melt and lose some of its coldness and then fed it to Alba. Her face lit up at the taste of the ice cream and she giggled, "Yay!" Other diners smiled tenderly at the grinning little girl.

I settled Alba into the warmth of the cot and kissed her, wishing her a final happy birthday. Our eyes were heavy with the drowsy contentment of a day in the sun. I nestled myself in the white sheets of the bed and started to close my eyes. Leo wrapped his arms around me and together, we drifted off to sleep.

In the morning, we let the last drips of water trickle out of our swimsuits and packed our suitcases. I took Alba down for breakfast while Leo checked that we had left nothing behind. After we had eaten, we went for one last walk along the coast.

Having strayed for too long along the beach, we ran to board our train – just making it in time. Leo and I heaved deep breaths in and out and Alba bounced up and down, extremely excited from the fastest ride she had ever experienced in her stroller. We collapsed into our seats and once recovered, chatted for the rest of the ride.

Chapter Seventeen

The months leading up to summer passed by in a happy blur. For Easter, Char, Mitch, baby Sean, Amelia and her girls, and Mom and Dad came to Florence for a week. Alba, instead of being the baby, became the big girl who adored playing with Sean. Amelia's girls danced around the two little ones like mother hens protecting their brood, playing with Alba's hair and helping select her clothing to match theirs and carefully holding Sean. Sean was four months old; Char blossomed with motherhood and Mitch was more lively and animated than ever, both luxuriating in the little utopia of their little family. Mom and Dad adored spending time with all their grandchildren and were happier than ever to enjoy special time together – especially over the holiday. Leo, Marina, Vince and their children joined our happy band as we explored Florence.

I took them to L'Osteria Di Giovanni and to less tourist-known sights like the Chiostro dello Scalzo, which was once a cloister and now has hazily beautiful frescos of the life of Saint John the Baptist, aged with the slight smile of light, in a courtyard square with sun streaming in and pillars holding up the walls. Green plants crept up the pillars, verdant among the faded beauty of its surroundings. It was a peaceful and fun week and it was fantastic to spend time together and let them get to know Leo better.

Kirsten and I had been in touch since the New Year and frequently went out for lunch or coffee. I gave her tips on weddings from my extensive reading on the subject for designing and from other weddings I had attended. She told me about how she had met Tommy and what they both liked and from that, I gave her suggestions. Sitting, drinking espressos, the hours with Kirsten passed quickly and with great fun. Alba would sit on my knee and Kirsten would make faces at her and play with her. "Tommy and I have decided to adopt children," she told me, "The world is too cruel and we want to be able to be able to change the life of at least one or two children." Her words touched my heart as I thought of the wonderful children that Aaron and I had met on our trip to care for children at an orphanage in India; I assured her, "That is an amazing thing to do."

After much conversation about her wedding, we got to the subject of Kirsten's wedding gown. She was hesitant to buy one because she wanted something special, something that she would be proud to pass on through her family, so she asked me to design and sew her gown. Although it would be my first time sewing a wedding gown from a design I drew, I was ready for a challenging diversion from the alterations and other work that I had been doing for almost a year. I altered the final garments that people needed and told my clients that I could not finish any new alterations until early July. We decided to work with chiffon. The dress we designed was ivory colored with a low-slung waist made of a sash of silver cloth. The neckline was heart shaped and led to a slender column from the breast to the waist. From the waistline, the cloth fell into a loose skirt that draped to the ankle.

On June first, my twenty-ninth birthday, Marina took Alba for the day while Leo and I went into Tuscany on his motorbike. I wore a leather jacket over a black tank top and denim capris with black wedge booties. Leo handed me a sleek black helmet and I strapped it over my head. My hands slid around Leo's waist and I leaned against him. When he sensed that I was comfortable, he turned on the engine and we barreled out into the street. We sped out of the city boundaries of Florence and into the rolling hills of Tuscany. The engine purred smoothly and Leo, knowing that I adored speed, went even faster. We flew past other cars on the autostrada and I whooped with exhilaration.

After about an hour, we arrived at the town of San Gimignano, a place sometimes called the 'New York of Tuscany' from its tall, "skyscraper" medieval towers and masses of tourists. We took off our leather jackets and folded them in the back of his bike. Leo ran a hand through his flattened curls as I tugged a brush through my wind-tangled hair. Finally ready, we walked up the stairs from the parking garage into the town.

Leo led me into a wine bar on the main square for lunch. We sat in a courtyard with twirling vines above our heads and ordered *bruschetta* and red wine. The sun filtered through the vines, playing with the color of the wine, making dancing pale reflections on the tables. When lunch was over, Leo held my hand as we walked through the winding streets. The mellifluously haunting music of a flute twisted through the air and we wandered the ancient alleys to find the musician. Sitting on the steps of a well near where he played, we let the music wash over us. Enchanted, I closed my eyes and let the music fill my mind. My eyes filled with tears as the beautiful music touched the most guarded parts of my soul. We listened and listened until the flautist stopped for a gelato break.

I tore myself out of the spell that the flute had cast over me and let Leo lead me in and out of shops and to an amazing little photography store near where we had parked. I stared in awe at the perfectly captured photographs of Tuscan sunrises and sunsets, day and night, snow and sun – every season in every landscape Italy had to offer. The photographer used light in the most creative ways to reflect yellow haze on fields, magnify purple skies over green bales of hay, and create black and white rivers of light through forests. After reflection, I chose a fifteen-euro print of a green-lit sunrise over rolling emerald hills covered in fog that Leo bought me as a birthday present.

The day turned to dusk and we sat down in a little restaurant in an alley. We ate simple and delicious Tuscan bean soup and *panzanella*. The cherry on top of a wonderful day, we ventured into a little store that held what had been voted the 'Best Gelato in the World.' I had a succulent cone with passion fruit, white chocolate, and Nutella flavored gelato. Leo decided on lemon, *stracciatella*, and *nocciola*. We sumptuously licked the creamy, rich dessert. Once finished, we put on our leather jackets and helmets again and headed back toward the autostrada. The wind pushed and shoved the hair that hung around my shoulders from the helmet and nipped at my cheeks.

The bike slowed to a stop in front of my apartment and Leo helped me off his bike. I tried to hand him the extra helmet but he stopped me with a smile and the wave of his hand, "No, it's yours. I bought it so that we can go out on my bike more often." He winked and put his arm around me as we walked upstairs.

It was days like that when I could completely understand the meaning of being drunk on life, full of its glory and happiness and love. I stopped Leo on a platform on the way up the stairs, pulled him close, and kissed him. "Thank you," I murmured, "for everything, for bringing me back to life and putting the sun back in my sky, for loving me, and for loving Alba."

He slipped a box out of his jacket, exactly as he had one year before. He placed it in my hands and upon opening it, the box revealed a delicately thin golden chain with a pure gold sun pendant whose rays twisted magnificently and a ruby shone from the center. Leo spoke clearly, "Last year I gave you the moon, this year I give you the sun, and I want you to know that you are the moon, the sun, the stars, and the world to me. I love you." My eyes grew wet and I wrapped my arms around him and gently pressed my lips to his.

We walked to Marina's apartment and he kissed me goodnight before saying goodbye. Marina relaxed in front of a fan at full blast with her feet on a cushion. "Ciao Nicolette," she waved and pointed at Alba playing with Bella on the ground. I gave her a hug, thanked her, and brought Alba back to our apartment to put her to bed. Sitting on the windowsill, my knees tucked under my chin, I gazed at the night sky, the stars twinkling and the moon smiling down on Florence. I tilted my head down to stare at my hand, contemplating the silver vine wedding ring that still adorned my left hand's ring finger. Slowly, I pulled it off into the palm of my hand and closed my fingers around it. I shut my eyes, my hand feeling naked and the ring burning into my palm, "It's time," I whispered, "The past is so very far away." I unlatched the necklace that held Aaron's ring and cautiously released my grip on my ring, adding it to the chain alongside its partner. I held the necklace for another moment and then refastened the clutch around my neck.

Chapter Eighteen

As Leo had promised, we planned a week-and-a-half long trip to Milan, Venice, and Rome. He, Alba, and I were going to leave in mid-June, the day after Kirsten's wedding. Kirsten and I finalized her dress, sewing the final stitches onto the embroidered, corseted top and helping her find the perfect shoes to match. When she tried it on during the last fitting, she turned around, seeing her reflection in the mirror and gasped. She shone, the dress falling from her in a perfect cascade. She grabbed me in a hug, "Thank you, Oh I love it!"

The morning of the wedding, Leo arrived, looking dapper in a dark blue suit and a pale yellow shirt. I dressed Alba in a flowing, sparkling pink dress and I put on a royal blue, high-low dress with an empire waist and deep blue wedges. I braided back the front of one side of my hair and put a small white flower in. I clipped a little, pink bow into Alba's dark hair. With Alba in one arm and Leo on my other, we walked to the Duomo. I saw Kirsten at the front and gave her a huge hug, "You look stunning!" I told her and she winked at me. She was a beautiful bride, glowing with happiness and grinning at her groom.

I spent most of the wedding ceremony walking with Alba up and down the back aisles of the Duomo. Alba smiled happily as long as we were not sitting. After the wedding, Kirsten had rented a fantastic grassy area under the Uffizi alongside the Arno. We danced, ate, and talked until midnight with the enthusiastic band playing and the never-ending buffet providing a little more fuel to those in need of dancing another dance. Kirsten had invited many people with children to the wedding, so she hired a babysitter who entertained them at a table while the adults danced. I left Alba with them and Leo invited me to dance. We spun across the dance floor, caught in the fancy-free frenzy and abandon that the music led us into. We danced another dance, and another, and another until our legs were weak from the exertion. I ambled over to where the babysitter held her court of children to find Alba sitting with another one-year-old, a little boy named Giuseppe Michelangelo - which was quite a long name for such a small, adorable child. They slid from their chairs and toddled around on the grass as they fell and giggled together. He tried to hold her hand and she swatted him away as his mother, who had also appeared, and I laughed happily. Leo, Alba, and I left, feeling bubblier and more alive than before.

I was up until three, finishing packing and making sure I had everything Alba and I would need: clothes, toiletries, food, and medicines. At eight, I dabbed on my final makeup, folded up Alba's stroller, and we got into Leo's taxi with a medium-sized black suitcase, shoulder bag, and purse. Once at the train station, we managed to maneuver our way through the crowded platforms and into our compartment on the train. We sat back and our eyes fell shut to the train's rhythm. Leo gently shook me awake as the voice resounding across the train called, "We have arrived in Milan." I grabbed sleeping Alba, her stroller, and a suitcase while Leo carried everything else and we jumped off the train as it pulled away from the station, chugging off to its next destination. "You look like a pack mule," I laughed as I took two of my three bags but Leo continued to carry the rest.

In Milan, we stayed with Leo's parents, Arabella and Francesco. They hugged Leo and me enthusiastically and picked up Alba, kissing her on the head and pinching her cheeks with a bright hello.

Arabella and Francesco took us walking around the city on two of our days there. Sadly, we didn't manage to get reservations to see Da Vinci's "The Last Supper" as the limited tickets had all been sold months before. One of the days, we were in a fashion district and I looked wistfully into the windows where designer mannequins sat gracefully, wearing stunningly stylish garments. I studied the careful stitches and was pulled into the fabric of the wisteria gown. We moved along, caught in the hurry to visit the Duomo, rushing past the alluring lights, catching the models in their glass cells.

On our final day there, Leo and I stared out of the windows at the glistening streets, caught entranced by the dancing rain falling like silver from the murky skies. Pulling on waterproof shoes and picking up vibrantly colored umbrellas, we laughed as we wandered out into the rain. Arabella, Francesco, Alba, Leo, and I made the most of our last day together: ducking in and out of museums, marveling at stores, and sitting in restaurants wrapped in the warm smell of tomatoes and wine.

We caught our train to Venezia Santa Lucia Train Station. Venice – the picturesque postcard of glittering canals and magnificent bridges – took my breath away. "A city you like?" Leo asked playfully. Struck speechless, I nodded. Leo laughingly called a water taxi for us. I did a tricky balancing act, clutching Alba to my chest with one arm and stepping onto the boat while the driver took my other hand. We managed to board the boat without falling in and settled ourselves at the sun-drenched open back of the boat. Leo, who had been to Venice many times, held Alba while I stood up from the leather seat and let the wind whip past me and the sun and salt warm my face and bare shoulders. I looked down at Leo as I tilted my head back, laughing with the pure joy of the moment. He grinned as I looked around with the excitement of a wide-eyed child.

All too soon, the purring engine of the boat quieted as we reached a dock by our hotel, a small bed and breakfast in a converted palazzo near St. Mark's Square. Once settled, we ventured out into the streets and explored countless bridges and alleys lining dark canals. Alba's stroller was difficult to maneuver through the crowds and up and down the stairs on bridges but working together, Leo and

I managed. Rather than sigh about the hordes of people, we laughed and continued our amble through the narrow, lively, and colorful streets of Venice. I gasped in awe at the designs of the bridges that had withstood the test of time, rising waters, and the wear and tear of tourists throughout history. Ghosts of the past shimmered on the walls, hovering, smiling at the future that their lives still mattered in. Sleek speedboats tore through the canals, maneuvered rather skillfully by their dark Italian drivers. Gleaming gondolas paraded through the canals, the bodies of their straw hatted drivers twisting as they plunged the paddle deep into the shadowy water. Accordions cried out from the gondolas of lovers, their bellows stretched in song, as their skillful owners crooned comparisons between the moon and pizza pies.

We spent two more days in Venice and we saw many of the tourist sights – the Rialto Bridge, the Bridge of Sighs, the Doges' Palace, the Guggenheim Museum, and various markets with Murano glass glimmering, fans fluttering, and masks eerily grinning as their limp ribbons tumbled onto the display cases. Sitting in St. Mark's Square, we paid the exorbitant prices for two glasses of wine and the pleasure of watching pigeons flutter around the square, listening to classical music boom from different platforms from women in black with violins embraced to their chests and men tightly tucked into tuxes cradling cellos, and observing the hordes of people and architecture around us. We also visited the less touristy areas in backlit alleys where little bridges with wrought iron rails dripping with pansies connected apartments and old men reminisced about the days, dames, and deeds gone by as they sipped espressos out of dainty cups. On our final afternoon, Leo took Alba and me to Burano, a rainbow of colorful houses on an island that was a short ferry ride from Venice. The houses were a bright assortment of colors with various items of clothing hanging between the buildings, and striped curtains draped across doorways waving like jolly flags. We munched on melting pizzas at a little restaurant near the main square as the purr of the air conditioning soothed our warm bodies.

We took a water taxi back to the train station where our Venetian adventure had begun to resume our travels on to Rome. Upon our arrival in the Eternal City, Leo flagged a taxi and stowed our bags in the trunk. When we arrived at the Roman bed and breakfast that lay at the foot of the Spanish Steps, the driver seemed to have overcharged us. Leo and the driver had a very verbal, very loud, very typically Italian argument. I covered Alba's ears and went to check in with the elderly lady who owned the place.

Leo came in to the bed and breakfast with a triumphant smile. Justice had prevailed and Leo had negotiated his money back. I looked outside to see the cabby fuming as he drove away.

We diffused the Roman heat with grainy lemon granitas, then walked to the Trevi Fountain and through the Travestere neighborhood. At the famous fountain so elaborately dotted with water spitting sculptures, Leo and I threw our coins in and in doing that – it was promised that we would return to Rome. We joked about the silly tradition but still engaged in it, hoping to reenter Rome many times in our future. Alba waved at almost everyone she saw from her perch in her stroller. At one point, she started to squirm and Leo took her stroller so she could walk with me while we gradually found our way through the throngs of people in the congested streets. I picked Alba up, afraid that she would stumble at an inopportune time, and we stopped to admire Bernini's Four River Gods Fountain in Piazza Navarro. The magnificent figures twisted and turned realistically under the mastered hands of Bernini. One blinded with cloth, another rotating to look out into the crowd, these symbols of power sat, unflinching against the test of time.

We had made a reservation to visit the Borghese gallery the next day and we rose early to go. The quarters of the imposing house brimmed with priceless, lavish works of art. We ambled from one grandiose room to the next in a trancelike state, struck in awe of the amazing collection by the Catholic Cardinal Scipione Borghese in the early seventeenth century. Everything from Caravaggio's dark, somber works depicting the bleakest side of human nature, to lighter pieces, featuring mythological beings overseeing the world from their heavenly perch, hung from the silken walls. Astounding sculptures took center-stage in almost every room, their faces conveying every emotion from fright to lusty desire.

After the magnificence of the gallery, we explored the lush gardens with trees filtering yellow light onto the dusty ground. Alba's feet pitter-pattered against the ground as she walked independently in front of me. She fell down onto a sun-splattered patch of pavement and gave me a look of immense surprise. She looked disdainfully at the path, put her hands down and pushed herself up into a standing position again and started to wander ahead. I looked at Leo and grinned, "She's becoming little Miss Independent, isn't she?" He laughed and nodded enthusiastically.

During our little Roman holiday, we went to visit the Vatican and to see the Vatican Museum. We were awestruck by the huge collection that was housed there and most of all by the remarkable Sistine Chapel. Jesus's fiery face and imposing hands, one ready to strike the masses and damn them and the other granting salvation, filled people of every nationality and age with awe – most especially the pope of the time, a dear foe of Michelangelo, who cringed and fell to the floor. The skinned body of Michelangelo at the hands of a martyr caused me to cringe, while Leo laughed at the donkey eared, snake bitten Cardinal who opposed Michelangelo and thus was forever captured in his Hell. We enjoyed a lunch of mozzarella and tomato *panini* in the beautiful courtyard with a glass of wine while a four-piece orchestra played Vivaldi.

On our last night in Rome, we ate at a romantic restaurant called The Library. The food was fantastic, ending with sumptuous chocolate lava cake. When we arrived back in Florence, Marina and her children were there to meet us at the station to welcome us home.

Chapter Nineteen

To thank Marina for all of the times she had watched Alba and been there for me, I offered to watch her children for two nights so she and Vince could have a little vacation before their new baby arrived. On that Friday evening, she brought them to my apartment where I had moved the couches and set up four sleeping bags. Gian, an energetic seven-year-old, Marco, a mischievous six-year-old, and Bella, the darling four-year-old, ran in the door shrieking, "Zia Nicolette, Zia Nicolette!"

On the first night, I taught them the joys of a s'more. They had never tasted marshmallows and they gobbled them down with blissful looks on their tan faces. After that, Bella and I played 'house' with Alba. Bella comically pretended to be the all-knowing older sister and I was their mother. All the while, Gian and Marco watched cartoons on T.V. At nine o'clock, Alba had already been put to bed in her crib and I decided it was time for the others to fall asleep. I helped Bella brush her teeth while Gian and Marco dressed in their pajamas.

Once everyone had been to the bathroom, brushed their teeth, and put on their pajamas, I led them to the sleeping bags I had laid out. They reluctantly wrapped themselves into little cocoons. Bella asked, "Can you tell us a story?" I gladly obliged with the story of Snow White, leaving out the scarier elements and focusing on the magical ones, and by the end Bella lay asleep, her thumb in her mouth, and the boys fought yawns. I lay down in my sleeping bag and feigned sleep. Finally, the boys were too tired to stay up any longer and drifted off to sleep.

The next morning, I woke up with the birds to feed Alba, rubbing my back from my unaccustomed night on the floor. The children wandered in as I finished feeding her and I made them waffles. I drizzled on Nutella and sprinkled a puff of powdered sugar over the top. They oohed and aahed for precisely two seconds before digging into the treat. Around ten, I sat with Alba on my lap, watching the kids draw pictures when Leo walked in. Gian and Marco leapt on him and he let them ride on his back like a horse around my apartment. "My turn, my turn!" cried Bella and Leo snatched her up and swung her around in the air, laughing and laughing. We took them for a walk over to the Duomo area and went on a horse and carriage ride. The boys made faces at everyone we passed while Bella waved like a princess and Alba looked around very keenly from such a new point of view.

They rode on the carousel, ate sweets and gelato, and were each allowed to buy one item they wanted from the market. Bella selected a bright magenta bracelet with the word Florence printed again and again around it. Marco chose a coin purse and Gian picked a postcard with the Ponte Vecchio on it. For dinner, the children ate *spaghetti alla carbonara,*

Alba enjoyed applesauce, I ordered a salad, and Leo chomped on a *panino*. When everyone had contently full stomachs, we walked back to my apartment and watched Disney's "Hercules" in Italian. Bella adored the movie, swooning at the songs and grinning at the love story between Megara and Hercules. Gian and Marco acted along, flexing their skinny arms in hopeful imitation of the charming Hercules. Leo sat, watching with an amused expression, clapped his hands as soon as it was over and said, "Okay children, to bed you go!"

He watched the boys get ready to make sure that they were not misbehaving while I put Alba to bed. Bella watched us very keenly. "I'm going have a baby girl someday too!" she exclaimed. I laughed quietly. Alba had fallen asleep, so I put her in her crib, took Bella's hand, and led her to the sleeping bags. The boys were sitting on top of theirs with Leo and when they spotted me coming, they wrapped themselves in the makeshift beds and lay down quickly. Leo got up as Bella stepped into her sleeping bag and I thanked him for spending the day with us.

I took them back over to Marina's apartment the next morning and she asked worriedly, "How did they behave? Were you able to handle them?" I grinned and told her that we had enjoyed spending time together, that we had a lot of fun, and that they had been perfect angels. She sighed with relief and I told her I would be happy to watch them again soon.

A few days later, Leo came over full of excitement. "Leave Alba with Marina, please come out with me tonight!" he pleaded and after I had agreed, he left to let me get ready. I kissed Alba goodbye at Marina's apartment and Marina also seemed to be teeming with excitement, she hinted, "Leo has some good news today!"

I was puzzled as I trekked over to L'Osteria Di Giovanni, where he had promised to meet me that night. I sat down and the owner greeted me cheerfully and said he had a table ready for us. The waiter poured two glasses of welcome prosecco and I sipped mine. Leo came bounding in through the doors as energetically as an excited schoolboy. He spotted me and sat across from me and took a gulp of the sparkling wine. "Leo, I can't stand the suspense! Just tell me already!" He winked, "Why don't I show you instead?"

He took a wrapped package that I hadn't noticed him carrying out from under the table. I raised an eyebrow and he nodded as I tore it open; the packaging revealed a book. There was a picture of the silhouette of a man standing against a large rock in front of a stunning sunset over a crystal clear sea. I looked up and he gestured for me to look down again. "*Finding Andromeda*, Leo Caviatolli." My mouth dropped open in shock as I jumped out of my seat to give him a hug. "Congratulations!" I exclaimed. He grinned widely, "This is the first copy. I promised you that you would be the first to receive one, and now you are!"

We sat there, smiling and smiling. I promised to start reading it the minute I arrived home. Leo talked about the whole process that had been such a secret and I learned about all of the challenges of writing, editing, translating, publishing, and printing. We parted late that night with a final kiss of congratulations. I rocked with Alba on Marina's rickety, wooden rocker so that she would drift off to sleep while Marina chatted about how excited she was for Leo's book. I excused myself so that I could go to start reading and put Alba, who had fallen asleep, in her crib.

The minute I started reading, I found I could not stop. It began with the voice of an old man, Luigi, reminiscing about his life. In his youth, Luigi had studied Greek mythology day and night and he connected stories of his past to those of the gods, the heroes, and the mortals. Of all of the tales in his life, the one he most loved was that of Andromeda and Perseus.

In the myth, Andromeda's mother had boasted that her daughter was more beautiful than the Nereids, the infamously gorgeous daughters of Poseidon. Enraged, Poseidon sent a sea monster to torture their city, the only way to save the city being to sacrifice Andromeda. Perseus, on his way back to his kingdom after beheading Medusa, saw a beautiful woman chained to a rock. He slayed the sea monster and married his lovely bride, Andromeda. After their deaths, they were placed among the stars as lovers for eternity.

Luigi followed that chronicle throughout his life, waiting to find, to rescue, and to love his Andromeda. But it was not he who found her – instead, she found him in some of the darkest moments of his life and, as he joked, Luigi became Andromeda and his love became Perseus. The last words said, "I have grown old, my Andromeda has been placed among the stars. Our love may have not been the greatest epic or tragedy of all time but I know that soon, the stars will dance and we will reunite, hung among the heavens forever." On the final page, were the words for the world to see, "This book was written for Nicolette, she is my guiding star, my Andromeda." I wiped tears from my face as I watched the darkness that heralded dawn.

The rest of July passed languidly and the days grew hotter and more humid. The breezes stifled the Florentines and filled the city with their damp heat. We ventured out later in the evenings as the pale sheen of the grown moon spread coolness across the city. Alba, Leo, and I rested on the Ponte Vecchio, listening to Claudio play the guitar on the worn cobblestones when the safety of night came. Alba happily played and tugged on the fur of patient small dogs that older couples brought on their walks. Alba sat on my lap during those blessed nights, reaching up to pat my face or pull my hair with clamped fists. We laughed and life was perfect.

Leo's book was met by great enthusiasm from the Italians who bought it and he was getting ready to release it in America and Britain. He travelled to various bookstores and new towns to talk about his book. We spent as much time as we could together when he was in Florence: going for walks, visiting little restaurants for lunch or dinner, and playing with Alba while chatting animatedly to each other.

SUNRISE

Chapter Twenty

At the beginning of August, Leo told me that he wanted to take me on a special date that evening. I jokingly checked my calendar while he stood in my kitchen and I laughed, "Looks like I have nothing going on." He gave me a cute half-smile and asked, "Can you leave Alba with Marina tonight? This night is just for you and me." We agreed that he would be outside my building at seven and I hugged him goodbye.

I fed Alba some cooked squash and then let her play with blocks on her blanket and nibble on Cheerios while I readied for a night out. I dried my hair most of the way, letting the ends curl the way I liked. After looking through my closet, I decided on a pair of black denim capris and a blue lace tank top, and put on my golden sun necklace Leo had given me for my birthday. I picked up Alba; she played with my necklace and I kissed her on either cheek, stroking her hair.

I handed Marina a bottle of milk to feed Alba later and exclaimed, "I love you Alba." "Ciao!" Alba cried. Marina hugged me and said, "Have fun darling." I took her hand, "Thank you so much for always helping me with Alba. Don't tire yourself, your baby will be coming soon." She smiled happily and said, "Don't worry my dear, I will be fine! Now go, enjoy yourself!" I grinned and ran downstairs with my helmet in one hand and leather jacket in the other.

Leo stood by his freshly gleaming Harley with a helmet in one hand and a small picnic basket in the other. He strapped on his helmet and I followed suit, admiring his sleek black helmet and leather-jacket covered form. He placed the little basket in the back of his bike and mounted the bike. I straddled the bike behind him and wrapped my arms around him. We drove onto the highway and he took an exit after a little while. When he braked, I recognized the lake in the countryside we visited the previous October. Leo spoke up, "I thought you'd like a break from the Florentine heat." He unfolded a blanket out of the back of his bike and unfurled it across the ground. I slipped off my shoes and tucked my feet under me as I watched him take out a cold glass bottle of prosecco, two tomato mozzarella *panini*, and lemon squares. I slipped my shoes off and put them on the edge of the blanket.

We talked about his trips to promote his book as we ate. By the time we were nibbling on the crumbling lemon squares, he was talking about his next book idea. The sun started to set; its final glowing reflections glittered on the lake's smooth surface. Leo got up to take the picnic basket back over to the bike. I went over to a recycling bin that was some fifty yards away and threw the glass bottle in. I walked back to find Leo pacing back and forth. He had left the blanket on the ground, but suggested we go for a walk on the edge of the lake.

Holding hands, we stumbled down the hill, laughing. We dipped our bare feet into the sun-warmed water. I dug my feet in the water-saturated sand and tried to hold my hair back from flying across my face in the increasing breeze. Leo looked at me with a serene, happy look on his face. His eyes sparkled and his curls were lightly tousled. He cuffed the legs of his jeans and waded in further to meet me. He held my hair back from my face with one hand and turned my face to meet his with the other.

As he pulled away, he released my hair, letting it fly around me once more. Leo took my hand and led me to a spot that was sheltered by a rocky ledge. The water gleamed hues of blue and pink as the sun's rays made their final appearance, bowing to the audience of day.

Leo grasped for something in his pocket, grinning certainly at me. I smiled at him when he dropped to the ground on one knee, holding open a black velvet box with a ring inside. "Nicolette, there was a time when I believed I would never find a love like Andromeda. The minute I met you, I knew that I was wrong. You are the most kind, loving, gentle, and beautiful person I have ever met. I love you with all of my heart, my soul, and my being. Will you marry me?"

Time slowed down and my breathing grew rapid. I stepped forward, wrapped my arms around him, and looked into his eyes, "Yes," then I kissed him and looked at him again, "Yes!" My hands shook as he slid the ring onto my finger.

We stood frozen in time as the granules of sand flew around us. He took my right hand and I looked at my left one. I peered at the ring for the first time; it was a slender white gold band with a gently sparkling trio of sapphires at the top. I hugged him, burying my face in his shoulder, the smile on my face growing. He took my hand.

We climbed back up the hill and lay down on the grass staring up at the stars. "There she is," I whispered, "There's Andromeda." His face crinkled in a smile, "It looks like I found my Andromeda, or perhaps my Andromeda found me." I laughed quietly, "We found each other." I rested my head on his shoulder and closed my eyes, one hand feeling my new ring in awe. When night had enveloped Tuscany and the stars were our sole guides, we slipped our shoes back on. Together, we folded the blanket and put it in the back of his bike. We fastened on our helmets and I whispered, "This seems so much like a fantasy that I almost don't want to go back to real life." Leo touched my cheek and murmured, "If you want, we can live in a fairy tale forever, as long as we are making it up together." I laughed, wrapped my arms tightly around his waist, and pressed my cheek to his back as we sped into the night.

We arrived back at the apartment building. "Together?" Leo asked and I replied, "Always." I grasped his hand and we walked up the stairs. Marina came to the door and slightly crankily said,

"Well you two are late tonight." "For good reason," I assured her and Leo exclaimed, "Marina, we're going to be married!" She exclaimed, "Oh my goodness! *Congratulazioni!*" causing her three children and husband to run into the living room as well as Alba to wake up.

I hurried to pick Alba up and she stopped crying the minute I held her. I cuddled her close and pressed my lips to her dark head. Vince and the children were in a commotion when they heard the news and Marina exclaimed with wink, "Well I guess since everyone is awake now, we'll have to celebrate." She went into the kitchen and took out some biscotti and a nearly full tub of gelato. And with Alba in one arm and Leo grasping my free hand, surrounded by our Italian family, we celebrated.

The next day, Leo and I called my mom when I knew she would be in her office before her day began. She smiled as soon as she saw our images on her screen, "Nicolette! And Leo! What a fantastic surprise!" We both exclaimed our hellos and Leo smiled as I cried, "We have some amazing news Mom, we're going to be married!" Her mouth dropped open and she exclaimed, "That's wonderful! I'm so happy for the two of you. I can fly over to help with the wedding whenever you want!" We laughed and Leo said, "We're not that far in the planning yet." She promised she would tell Dad and we hung up, assuring we would send more details later.

Amelia was extremely pleased and Char laughed with happiness, "Oh Nicolette, you couldn't deserve this more."

The hardest call I would make was to Stacy; I knew that even when I first dialed her number. We greeted each other and as we spoke, I told her that Leo and I were engaged. Tears flooded her Adriatic eyes for a moment, and then slowly her lips folded upward in a serene smile. "I am so happy for you my dear," she murmured. Then, more loudly, she said, "I wish you the greatest happiness."

Chapter Twenty-One

On August eighteenth, Marina's fourth child, a little girl, was born. They called her Erika Genesia. Leo, Alba, and I stood by as Marina smiled, hearty even after the trials of giving birth. "By the fourth birth," Marina laughed, "it becomes far easier my dear." We laughed as Marina's three other children leapt over one another to sneak a peek at their sister. Little Bella looked ready to start jumping up and down on her mother's hospital bed in her joy to no longer be outnumbered by boys, her wish of having a sister finally fulfilled.

Leo and I went wedding ring shopping together a few days after Erika's birth. A friend watched Alba for us, wishing us swift luck in finding 'the ring.' We went to a small jeweler off the main streets. Within minutes, we identified the perfect rings. Mine was a slender white gold band while Leo's was slim and yellow gold. We paid and Leo slid them into his pocket to take home for safekeeping.

Hand in hand and having the whole evening to ourselves, we walked across the river to the foot of the hill and into our favorite pasta restaurant, Zeb. Seated around a gleaming glass bar with cheeses and meats displayed proudly, we ordered spaghetti with black truffles and two glasses of white wine. The glasses glinted in the pale lights, ringing with our laughter and conversation on the wedding and how I hoped to grow my home-run business into my own small shop. Olive oil slicked across our lips in a clear kiss and the dark, earthy tendrils of truffle melting on our tongues, we smiled in contentment with the magic drifting around us, the magic of love and of life and of food shared with the ones we love.

Leo and I decided that we wanted a simple wedding with only our closest friends and family. I told him how I had dreamed of a wedding by the lake where he had proposed, just as the sun's rays turned the sky pink with its setting. He kissed me and laughed, "You are a poetic soul Nicolette." We planned that Alba and I would move into his apartment after the wedding. I called my landlady and made the necessary arrangements for moving out by the date she asked me to leave. This new date rushed our wedding plans quite a bit.

Leo and I set the date for the twenty-ninth of September after talking to Leo's friend, Luca, who was a priest and willing to do a wedding outside because as he simply stated, "God is everywhere, and most especially He is in nature." My mother put her most trusted employee in charge of her company and flew to Florence to help. Arabella arranged the wedding dinner at an *agriturismo* – a local farm that cooks from their produce. For the rehearsal dinner, we made a reservation at L'Osteria Di Giovanni.

Mom, Alba, Marina, Erika, and I went shopping for a wedding dress, as I would have no time to make one for myself. We visited all of the traditional stores for wedding gowns, but no dress was quite right. Finally, after exhausting Florence's small bridal boutiques, we walked into a fancy dress shop. On one of the racks, a silvery dress peeked out. I strode over to it and gently plucked it off the hanger. I strolled into a changing room and gingerly put it on. The dress was strapless and rippling silver with a corseted bodice from underneath my breasts to my hips. There was a subtle design of vines in a lighter silver thread coming from the delicately cascading waist. I walked out and simply stated, "This is the one." Alba shrieked, "Yay!" while Mom's eyes started to tear up, and Marina smiled, "Yes, my dearest friend, that is most definitely the one."

I hung it in my closet and spotted the perfect pair of shoes to go with the dress. They were silver, three-inch heels with a strappy front and little crystals on the straps. Mom stayed with me, sleeping on the couch. Arabella called from Milan every day to talk about wedding plans, excitedly asking me my thoughts on this and that. Char came with Mitch and Sean on the twentieth. She, Amelia, and Marina were to be my bridesmaids. Leo's best men were two jovial, kind men who he had roomed with in college and all three had gone on to be professors. One of them, Rossario, a Sicilian, taught art history while the other, Paolo, a Florentine, taught Italian literature.

As the wedding day approached, I began to move my things into Leo's apartment. Some belongings, like my excess furniture and kitchenware, I put into storage. We fixed a room for Alba, leaving only her crib at my house until the last possible moment. I took photos of the paintings I had made on Alba's bedroom walls in my apartment, and Leo helped me to paint over them with thick, creamy paint as Paola had wished. Leo was going to take a week off work in early October to take me on a mystery honeymoon.

The wedding day came closer. On the twenty-sixth of September, Arabella and Francesco arrived, as did Dad, Amelia, her children, Stacy, and John. Mom, Leo, Alba, and I went to meet them at the airport and embraced them, receiving excited hellos and sincere congratulations. We took them to their hotel and promised to meet them later that evening for dinner.

After dinner, Leo came back to my apartment with me. Mom and Dad, who were both staying at my apartment, suggested, "Why don't we take Alba for a bit so that you can spend some time together?" Leo and I walked out of the apartment, giddy at the escape from the time-consuming planning. Ambling across the Ponte Vecchio, we hiked up to the monastery – lungs burning after our excited banter about the wedding, books we were reading, art, and the steepness of the hill. While our throats ran dry with the exercise, the conversation flowed easily.

The darkness of the church took a minute to clear, revealing the green marbled ground glinting silently and the faded, pastel images of saints and bishops adorning the faded walls. A rounded pyramid of candles flickered gaily, stars wavering from red tin hearts that pound with the wishes and prayers of the masses. Reverently, we knelt, the gnarled wood of a pew rippling beneath our fingers. I looked at him, his head tilted forward and jaw slack, his eyes closed in prayer and lashes a dark smolder on his cheek. I leaned over and rested my head on his shoulder, thanking God for the opportunity of our life together.

On the day of the rehearsal dinner, I started to feel butterflies in my stomach. Alba seemed to know that I felt nervous and spent longer than she usually would on my lap and gave me a big kiss before stumbling away. I dressed her first because I knew that would be easier than choosing something for myself. She wore a pale blue dress with little bows on it and a cloth headband with a big royal blue bow on it. I picked Alba up and sat her on a little stool in the closet. She said, "Mama," and climbed off the stool. She walked over to me, one little foot tumbling over the other. My heart lightened at her adorable smile as she planted a kiss on my cheek and ran away. After much looking, I decided on a golden colored dress with a fluttering hem and cut reminiscent of the roaring twenties. I fastened the sun necklace that Leo had given me around my neck.

Leo arrived at eight and took my hand as we walked to the restaurant. He carried Alba the whole way. Alba and Sean sat perched in high chairs and Erika snoozed in a baby carriage next to her mother. Alba animatedly spoke gibberish sprinkled with bits of Italian and English to Sean and he responded just as enthusiastically, maintaining an idyllically unaware conversation. Amelia's children watched over their younger cousins, feeling very sophisticated in their twirling laughs and dancing conversation. Arabella and Francesco happily chatted with my parents and Stacy and John.

The wine flowed freely and the conversation bubbled. The table maintained its jovial mood and at ten, the women of the family ushered me out, saying that I needed my beauty sleep. Laughing, we wandered down the street arm in arm, joking and talking, our joy flitting into the skies with light wings.

Chapter Twenty-Two

I woke to the rising sun, her gentle rays spreading into the sky, bringing life to the world. I slowly stepped out of bed with a smile as I thought about the day ahead. I strolled into Alba's room and picked her up, whispering, "Our new life begins today my darling!" Her bright blue eyes, so much like her father's, opened drowsily and a lazy smile crossed her mouth. I hugged her close and then decided to let her sleep for a while longer. She drifted off and I watched the sun finish its way into the sky. I lay back down but couldn't go back to sleep; my thoughts turned to Leo and my smile widened.

Around midday, Char and Mom came with me to purchase a bouquet. We looked at the myriad flowers and finally, I picked a beautiful bouquet arranged with sprays of baby breath and purple heather peeking out from between white lilies speckled with yellow and pink, irises, and white roses. We gasped at its magnificent, fresh fragrance, smiling at their innocent beauty. I also bought bouquets of red roses for Sunny, Helena, and Avril to throw single roses onto the aisle as the flower girls.

I stepped into the shower in my apartment for the last time. I closed my eyes under the warmth of the water and stood there for a few minutes.

Amelia, who had worked as a beautician during college, came in to help me paint my fingers and toes silver.

We ate a lunch of delicate finger sandwiches and then I excused myself to dry my hair. It fluttered past my chin, slightly curly, and when it was dry, Char, who possessed an expert hand at hair, helped me to loosely pull the sides back and secure them with curved silver pins. We left the short, wavy pieces that framed my face out of the pins. Char lightly fluffed the rest of my gently curling hair. As I stared at myself in the mirror, my bright green eyes peered back at me. There was no longer question or worry in those eyes but instead happiness and inner serenity. I smiled the slightest of smiles and my face lifted immediately.

Helena, Avril, and Sunny played with Alba and I could hear their laughter from where I sat, holding my mom's hand like a little girl. Stacy told me, "Your Leo seems like a good man, Aaron would have liked him. I wish you all happiness in your future." I leapt up and hugged her in relief; she had been so quiet the whole trip but in that moment, I knew she accepted my decision.

Alba grinned and gurgled happily as I dressed her in a purple, short puffy sleeved dress with white flowers embroidered just above the waist. I put a purple bow in her hair and lifted her into the air and spun around. I swept her down and kissed her forehead before sitting her on the ground with her toys. Helena, Sunny, and Avril walked out in matching pink, spaghetti strap dresses with tulle bands around their waists, ending in a big bow. "Don't you girls look pretty!" I exclaimed as Avril and Sunny nodded enthusiastically while Helena grinned, "It's pink." I laughed as Amelia came out, wearing a pretty, long burgundy skirt, black shimmering tank top, and black heels. "I love your idea of no bridesmaid's gowns!" she proclaimed as Char walked out in a maroon colored dress. Finally, Marina walked into the apartment in a dark blue dress. Mom and Stacy were already dressed in their outfits, Mom in a beige pants suit and Stacy in a dark pink skirt and jacket.

Grinning, I decided that it was time for me to get ready so I left the ladies in the living room to chat. I took down my dress, fluttering as gracefully as a lone butterfly, emerging from the chrysalis of my now empty closet. I slipped off my robe and stepped into the unzipped dress. I slid it up my body and zipped it up. I walked out in my dress, smile radiant on my face. The girls started to clap and the adults followed suit, whooping and whistling. "Now spin for us," Mom asked. I lifted my arms and spun in a circle. "You look beautiful!" Amelia beamed. Mom looked a little misty eyed as she murmured, "Perfect, just perfect."

I fastened the crescent moon necklace Leo had given me for my twenty-eighth birthday around my neck and stepped into the silver heels. Stacy took the bouquet out of the vase and after letting the water drip off the stems and carefully patting them down with a towel, tied a silver bow around it and handed it to me. I murmured, "Thank you Stacy, for everything." She kissed my cheek and my mom took my hand to step into the car for the trip to the lake.

Chapter Twenty-Three

The drive seemed to pass in a blink, sitting, listening to the voices that swirled around me in an almost surreal manner. As we stepped out of the car and onto the grass at the top of the hill, I saw the men and other children starting to take their spots on the beach. Helena, Sunny, and Avril clutched the roses firmly, not wanting to lose them to the breezes that tempted and turned the naïve heads of the blushing red roses. Like the girls, I held my bouquet close, calming myself with the aromatic perfume of the flowers that seeped into the air around me. The women led me down to an area crowded by trees in close proximity to the beach. My bridesmaids waited with me, hugging and kissing me. Arabella hurried over to me and grasped both of my hands, "My dear, I am so happy to welcome you into our family."

My father came into the area and looked at me proudly. In the gruff voice men use to conceal tears, he said, "Oh Nicolette, my baby girl, you are so beautiful. I'm going to have to let you go all over again. I love you so much." I hugged him. I lightly wiped my eyes and he took my arm.

The sky turned pink and the candles softly glowed as Gian walked down the aisle with the rings on a silver pillow. Helena followed, solemnly throwing roses to the ground. Avril and Sunny followed, slightly more light heartedly than Helena, letting the roses fly into the air before they softly dropped onto the sand. The best men, Rossario and Paolo, flanked Leo, smiling encouragingly. Amelia, Marina, and Char followed the flower girls.

The wedding march began to play and my father and I stepped forward in tandem, candles sparkling around us. I did not see a single face but Leo's, as I seemed to float above the rose strewn ground. He pressed a hand to his mouth, staring at me with wet eyes. I could feel the presence of Aaron in the winds, merging my past and my present as I walked forward. In the setting sun that lay ahead of me, I could see Leo and our life together. The sun's final rays illuminated Leo's face and I stood next to him. My father kissed my cheek and Father Luca began the Mass. The wind whirled around us and somehow, the candles refused its luring embrace to darkness. The sun dozed off, her eyes shutting a little more with every second, each shimmering lash fluttering across the sky's rosy cheek. She still shone radiantly in her dusk, her eyes dancing one final time with the life of light that she carried through the days and the nights, the bad and the good. Even when disappearing into the shadows of the mountains, she carried with her the spark – the spark that would light the world aflame with a new day and a new chance. The dancing words of the Mass spun into the air, hanging over the impending darkness, carried out to our family and friends. I listened closely and Gian stepped into his place and held the rings aloft with great pride. I picked up

Leo's ring and looking into his bright eyes, slid it onto his finger with the perfect words, promising our future. Leo picked up my ring and before he slid it onto my finger, I saw a single word engraved on the inside, flickering in the dusk.

It read, "Sunrise."

About the Author

An avid traveller, lover of Florence, and art enthusiast, Heather Keleher is a native of Raleigh, North Carolina.

Contact her at heatherkeleher.com.